PLAY *Me*

CARY HART

*Starr -
Cheesy pickup lines are the only kind!!!
xoxo*

Copyright

Disclaimer. This is a work of fiction. Names, characters, places, brands, media, and incidents are either a product of the author's imagination or are used fictitiously; any resemblance to actual persons living or dead, business establishments, events or locations is entirely coincidental.

The author acknowledges the trademarked status and trademark owners of various products referenced in this work of fiction. Any trademarks, service marks, product names or named features are assumed to be the property of their respective owners, and are used only for reference. There is no implied endorsement.

This book contains material protected under the International and Federal Copyright Laws and Treaties. Any unauthorized reprint or use of the material is prohibited. No part of this book may be reproduced, stored in a retrieval system, or transmitted in any form, or by any means, electronic, mechanical, photocopying, recording or otherwise, without prior permission of the author. For more information regarding permission email caryhartbooks@gmail.com

Cover designed by **Passion Creations by Mary Ruth**
Editing provided by **Dani Hall** of **DMH Editing Services**
Proofreading provided by **Marla Esposito of Proofing with Style**

Publication Date: May 10th, 2018
Paperback ISBN: 978-1718654693
Play Me (Spotlight Collection, #1)
Copyright ©Cary Hart 2018
All rights reserved

Books by Cary Hart

Battlefield of Love Series

Love War

Love Divide

Love Conquer

Spotlight Collection

Play Me

Protect Me (September 2018)

Make Me (January 2019)

Own Me (2019)

The Forever Series

(Coming November 2018)

Building Forever

Saving Forever

Broken Forever

Finding Forever

Hotline Collection

(Coming 2019)

Dedication

To anyone who is struggling with forgiveness... This one is for you.

Playlist

Play Me – Spotify Playlist

Trouble by Elvis Presley
Human Nature by VACAY
Music by JoJo
DNA by Lia Marie Johnson
Wasted by MKTO
Piece by Piece by Kelly Clarkson
Worth It by Danielle Bradbery
Rescue You by Johnnyswim
Stone by Alessia Cara
Never Be the Same by RUNAGROUND
1200 Days by Erick Baker
Wanna Hear Your Voice by Taps
Small World by Idina Menzel
American Man by Jake Scott
Can't Help Falling in Love by Haley Reinhart

Chapter One
Ellie

I play because I love it, it's in my blood. It's why I'm here today. Risking it all to do the one thing that saves me from myself. *Music.*

My own personal therapy. My only escape from the reality that surrounds me.

I need it more than I need air to breathe. Without it, I'm lifeless. A shell of the person I know I am meant to be.

Why can't they see that?

"Hey, El." The voice behind me saves me from the thoughts that have been consuming my time. The anticipation of "what-if's" has my nerves on high alert.

Turning, I see Jen, the barista at the local coffee shop Java Talk, holding out my beverage of choice: hot ginger tea with two teaspoons of honey. "Looks like you're closing out tonight."

"Thanks." I take the cup, my trembling hand showing what is hiding behind the walls I'm carefully trying to construct before *he* comes and tries to knock them down again. Destroying everything I'm trying to become. Everything I have always wanted to be. *Just me.*

"Whoa! What's with that?" She nods at the cup as I bring it toward my lips, giving it a quick blow. "No need, room temp." Jen smiles. "Wouldn't want you to burn those pretty pipes."

"Thanks." I take a quick sip, appreciating the warmth of the tea as it helps loosen my vocal cords.

"Is that the only word you know tonight?" Jen leans against the counter, crossing her arms.

"What?" I take a step back and lean against the half wall that separates the counter from the front door. The farther I get from her, maybe the less she will notice.

This moment, right now—tonight, it's more than just getting up in front of a crowd. No, *that* I can do. This is about independence and my lack of it. This is me standing tall, making a stand and fighting back. A declaration of the war I'm about to fight.

"Girl, *every* word out of your mouth has been 'thanks.' Which is cool and all, you know, because I'm all about manners and stuff, but that trembling hand." She moves forward, placing both hands on the counter that divides us. "You got the shakes bad and I'm willing to bet it has less to do with our makeshift stage over there," she throws her thumb over her shoulder, "and more about something else." She narrows her eyes, waiting for me to spill it.

"I just have a lot on my mind," I say evasively.

I should have known Jen would notice something was wrong. We've become close the past few months when I sneak home once a month to play Java Talk's Coffee Shop Acoustic Sessions.

"Well, it's a good thing you are here then. Baristas, we are a lot like bartenders." Jen's lips are pursed, eyes wide, as she nods, her suggestive salesman training in full effect. "Wanna tell me about it?"

That does it. Something breaks and I bend over in laughter. The look on her face and her trying to sell me therapy like she is selling the featured pastry of the month is too much.

Throwing her hands up she asks, "What? What's so freakin' funny?"

"It's just…" I try to catch my breath. "You." I push myself off the wall, exhaling out the laughter. "You're just funny. That's all." I walk past her, shaking my finger. "I needed that. Thank you."

She follows me from behind the counter. "I don't get it."

"Make that face again and look in a mirror." I gesture toward the reflective window behind her. "You looked so damn serious."

"I was serious." Jen turns around and makes the exact same face. Her eyes wide, she turns back around.

I chuckle. "You get it now?"

She picks up a towel and throws it in my direction. "Whatever. See if I ever try to help you again."

"You helped me more than you realize." I pick up the towel and hand it back to her.

Grabbing it out of my hands she dips it in the sanitizer and begins to wipe off the counter. "Mmm-hmm."

"Ohhhh come on now, don't be mad. It was a cute face."

Jen stops mid-cleaning and looks up. "It looked like I was constipated, trying to take a dump!"

"That too."

"Thanks for the boost of confidence. I'd rather have cute than…"

The bells over the front door, announcing the crowd that is about to come through. It's my cue to let the master get to work. Who am I to come between a customer and their coffee?

"Looks like you are getting ready to get hit. I think I'm just going to hang out here until my turn. That okay?"

"Yup." She braces herself for the rush of people.

Pulling out a stool, I settle in and wait for my turn, losing myself in the lyrics of the soft melody of the artist currently on stage.

"Is this seat taken?" The low rumble of a voice startles me from my music-induced trance.

Looking down the row of empty stools, I reply, "That is a piss poor excuse for a pickup—" I whip around in the stool and right into the chest of the most gorgeous guy I have ever seen. Tall, dark and hair slicked back like he just got out of the shower.

Don't go there.

I beg myself to fight the urge to lean toward him and breath in his scent. I'm pretty sure he will smell of all kinds of yummy.

"Rest assured, that wasn't a line." He seems a little amused. "If it was, I would say my game was way off."

"I'm the only one sitting here." I wave around to all the empty seats at the bar. Even though it's a special night, most of the patrons sit at the tables closer to the entertainment. "So, forgive me for thinking otherwise."

"I'm just waiting for my coffee. Wanted to stick close to the front without blocking the counter." He pulls out the seat. "So, may I?"

"Um, sure?"

"Are you?" He looks around. "Because I'm getting the feeling someone is occupying this seat."

"Yeah. I mean, no one is sitting there." I quickly turn back around, mouth agape from just making an ass out of myself.

"I'm going to have to ask you to leave. You're making the other girls look bad." His voice a seductive whisper, tickling all my senses.

Turning around once again, I come face-to-face with this beautiful stranger. His lips, so close to mine, turn up into a grin.

"What?" His proximity steals my breath away.

"*That* is a pickup line."

"Come again?"

"Pickup line." He leans back in his seat. "If I were to use one, I would have said that. Not 'is this seat taken?'"

"Lame." I somehow manage to break the spell.

"How do you figure? I had you. Hook, line and sinker." He winks.

"Dude, you are so wrong!" I hop up, grabbing my tea. "That ranks up there with 'Are you a time traveler? Cause I can see you in my future.'"

"Oh come on. It wasn't that bad."

"What's bad?" Jen slides his order down the bar, then stands there waiting for one of us to answer.

"Uhh…"

"Well…" he begins to explain. "I was just…"

"Oh my God! Grab a booth." She waves over to one that is being cleaned off. "Your secretive conversation is distracting me."

"You are a mess." I turn and head to the booth. As I slide in I notice hot guy is still sitting at the bar. "Are you coming or not?" I call to him.

Slowly standing, hot guy grabs his drink and walks right past me. *Seriously?*

Turning in the booth I see him change direction and come back, stopping right in front of me.

"Excuse me, miss. When I was walking by, I noticed you staring, so what's up?" He stands there looking all delicious, hands in his pockets.

"I wasn't staring…" The light bulb goes off. "Please tell me you don't really use that line?"

"Of course I do." He winks, taking a seat across from me.

"Whatever happened to just a simple introduction?"

"Now, why didn't I think of that?" He reaches across the booth, holding out his hand. He nods. "This is where you take it and I introduce myself."

"Huh?" I can't help but mess with him.

"See. Clearly my point. It doesn't work." He starts to pull back, but the urge to reach out and touch him overpowers my need to be a smart-ass.

"Ahhh, or maybe it does?" He gives my hand a little squeeze and shake. "I'm Lee Scott, construction worker."

Interesting. Explains the rough hands.

"I'm Ellie." I pause for a moment before I let the words tumble out of my mouth. "Ellie Thorne."

"Well, Ellie, Ellie Thorne. What's your story?" He retracts his hand, grabs the steaming cup of joe and leans across the table, seemingly interested in my every word.

"I'm actually quite boring." Which is true, for the moment.

"Oh, come on." Lee tilts his head to the side, daring me to tell him more. "Pretty young woman like yourself, there has to be more."

"I'm just a typical twenty-three-year-old college student who still doesn't know what she wants in life. I've dropped out of college at least two times only to be forced to go back by my overbearing parents." I bring my now cold tea to my lips, watching Lee from over my cup as I take a drink.

"I wouldn't worry too much about it. Sometimes it's hard to figure out what we want in life, until we get to experience it a little." Lee speaks with confidence. "It will come with time."

"See…" I set the cup back down and this time I'm the one finding myself entranced, leaning into his words. "That's the thing. How do you experience it? I have no idea what I want to do or what I'm *allowed* to do."

"What's your major?"

"Business law."

"Really? I wouldn't have figured you for the type." He leans back, examining me. "I mean, you do seem a little feisty." He winks. "But attorneys are brutal and you seem like the opposite."

"You're very observant, Mr. Scott."

"Very much so, Miss Thorne."

I wince.

"What's that look for?"

I could tell him the truth, but tonight is about living. Tonight is about my escape and Lee is just that for me, but there is something about him that makes me want to unravel it all.

"It's just so formal. That's all."

So much for unraveling.

"Ellie, let's lose the formality." He takes our cups and signals for Jen to bring us another round. "I came in here to grab a cup of coffee before I met a few friends for drinks." He glances at the time. "Which I'm late for and you know what?"

"What?"

"I don't care." Lee reaches for his cell and fires off a text as he continues. "I'd rather be here," he slides the phone back into his pocket, "with you. So, tell me everything or nothing. Either way, I'm not going anywhere."

Is it that simple?

"You go first," I counter.

"All right, I'm twenty-four, have a stable job with great benefits. My mom left when I was younger and I was raised by my grandparents, whom I like to think did a fantastic job. My grandfather had a passion for woodworking and taught me everything he knew."

"School?"

"Unfortunately, I didn't have the opportunity. My grandfather passed away when I was seventeen and I promised I would take care of my grandmother. So, I went to work."

"Do you regret it?" I question, needing the answer. Because regret consumes me daily. If I follow my dreams, I have regret. If I don't, then I have regret.

What I did today? I feel relief. But will regret soon follow once I suffer the repercussions?

"Sometimes, but it's not what you think. I always knew I wanted to work with my hands. So, regretting working in construction?" He pauses before continuing, "No. But wishing I could have taken a few courses in business, so one day I could start my own company? Yep. Every day."

"It's not too late. They offer online classes."

"I've thought about it, but right now, life is a little complicated." He reaches for his phone. "Speaking of which…" He scrolls through his messages and smiles.

Complicated.

A simple word that means so much.

"Girlfriend?" I blurt.

"Grandmother," Lee responds, flipping his phone, to show me a picture of an older woman holding up her pill box, with the lid off, all the contents emptied into her open mouth, her middle finger more visible than the rest. "She sometimes forgets to take her meds. I guess the talk I gave her yesterday worked."

"Now, *she* seems like a feisty one."

"That is an understatement." He throws his head back in a fit of laughter before he brings his eyes back down to meet mine. "So, about you?"

"I have two parents who have always controlled my every move. I've never had a real job. I love music. I'm addicted to vanilla-flavored ChapStick and all things lemon." I pause to gauge his reaction.

He confessed he had to work to support his grandmother and I basically tell him I freeload off my parents.

"Go on." He reaches across the table, covering the fist I didn't know I was making with the palm of his hand. As he slowly pries it open, the tension is freed from my body.

He smiles and removes his hand.

I smile and wish he'd put it back.

"Well, there is one thing that I love. It's actually why I'm here tonight—"

"Here you go." Jen hands Lee a refill then turns to me. "I know you don't like more than one cup before you go on and, well… you're up." She pats me on the shoulder before walking off.

"I'll be right back. I just have to do this one thing." I get up, pulling my ChapStick from my back pocket, applying it as I always do before I hit the stage. "It's only a couple songs."

"Songs?"

"I'll be back in about ten minutes." I turn around and head toward the coffee bar where Jen is waiting with my guitar.

"Looks like word traveled fast." She points at the doors. "I may have tweeted it."

"Jen!" I didn't want an audience tonight. The last thing I need is for my parents to find out I'm back in town.

"They are your fans, El. Don't try to hide from them."

Rolling my eyes, I grab the guitar and head to the stage, but not before looking back to see Lee standing, leaning against the wall.

Opening the worn leather case, I wrap my hand around the neck of the guitar and carefully lift it out while I take a seat on the stool.

Glancing up, I give Lee a quick wave, which he returns, before I speak into the microphone. "Testing, one, two, three." I slide the strap over my head, strum the strings and begin to belt out a crowd favorite.

Everyone is singing along and clapping their hands. The tempo is a little too upbeat for the atmosphere, but I love it.

I crave it.

This is who I was born to be. I can feel it, and even though they deny it, *they* know it too.

I decide that since I'm closing out and the audience is liking where this is going, I'm going to end it on a high note.

Adjusting the mic, I bring it closer and say, "A certain someone asked me what I wanted out of life." I scan the crowd to see him closer to the door now. "Ah, there he is." I flash him a smile. "Anywho, I may not know what I want out of life, but I do know what I want tonight..." I begin to play the few chords to Elvis Presley's "Trouble." "That's right. Trouble. Lee?" I settle in, strumming a few more chords. "What do you say? You wanna get into some trouble?" His face suddenly drops.

I must have embarrassed him.

"It's okay." I mouth before I start the song, one of my mom's favorites. Except Lee looks anything other than fine. Bouncing from foot to foot, I can tell, even from here, he's uneasy. That putting him in the spotlight was the wrong move because he does the one thing I didn't expect. He lowers his head, turns and walks out the door.

Plastering on a smile, I let the crowd carry me through the last note then swing my guitar over my back and run after him to apologize.

"Lee! Wait!" I push my way through the crowd, hoping I can catch up to Lee and convince him to stay. "Lee!" I'm almost to the door, but someone steps around the corner and damn near knocks me backward.

"Trouble? Seems fitting enough." He catches me by the arm a little too tightly.

This is what I didn't want to happen.

This is why I didn't announce I was back home.

This is why I have no choice but to do what I have to do.

"Father."

"Time to go home." He begins to pull me out the door.

"I have to get my case." I jerk back.

Reaching over my shoulder, he lifts the guitar over my head and hands it to someone behind me. "You're done! Do you hear me?"

"Don't you even think about it. That's mine," I hear Jen say as my dad pulls me out the door.

"I have my car." I break free and head toward my Mercedes, a high school graduation present from my parents, and climb in.

"Straight home, Eloise!" My dad walks by, tapping my hood.

This is where I want to shout back that I'm twenty-three years old. I'm an adult who can make my own decisions, but we both know that's a lie. I tried to live my life for me and when I did, he followed and always brought me back *home*.

Slamming the door, I tilt my head back and scream. "I can't do this!" I pound my fist against the steering wheel. I'm so caught up I'm unsure if I just laid on the horn or if my screams were that loud. Either way, I have onlookers.

Tonight felt good.

Tonight, *he* made me believe I could be anyone. Someone other than the person I pretend to be.

Chapter Two

Lee

One Month Later

"Move out of the way!" Niki pushes through our little party to make her way to the spotlights. "If I miss Kyle finally proposing to her, I will castrate you, fry up your balls and serve them as an appetizer. Your friends will be feasting on your balls, Scott." She walks backward, not taking her eyes off me.

"Dude, don't make eye contact." Gavin Sanders, the manager of Spotlight and Niki's husband, walks past me, wrapping an arm around her waist. "Here, babe." He hands her a fifty. "Let's get the spotlights going."

"Gavin?" She still continues to eye me while she slides the fifty into the slot, activating the beam. "Have you ever had Rocky Mountain oysters?" An evil grin appears on her face, but it quickly disappears as the crowd begins to shout that Kyle is down on one knee.

"Niki is all bite." Jen walks up behind me and hands me a beer.

"That's what I'm afraid of." I clink our longnecks together. "To happy endings — cheers."

"Oh my God! This has to be one of the most romantic proposals ever!" Jen sighs.

"I'm not sure how romantic it is having everyone blinding you with beams of lights while you are trying to propose to the love of your life. Kind of seems a little impersonal to me."

"Take that back!" She turns around, leaning against the railing, shooting me a death glare.

"Not a chance," I tease.

"I'm going to ignore that." She takes a step forward and pokes me in the chest. "But what I can't ignore is the fact you haven't been to Java Talk for almost a month."

"Should I be concerned?"

"About what?"

I take a long pull before I tilt the bottle in her direction. "Your stalker tendencies."

"Shut your mouth, Lee!" She slaps me on the arm.

"Here comes the happy couple!" Gavin announces to the party. "Scott? Where are you, man? Kyle says you have the next round."

"Come on, you are being summoned." She grabs my empty bottle and sets it on the table for the waitress to pick up.

"Right behind you," I start to say, but stop in my tracks when I hear her.

That voice.

"Lee, everyone is sitting down."

"I'm going to use the restroom." I quickly pass by her and head toward the stairs.

"Dude, we're in VIP. They are right over there."

"Shit!"

"Ohhhhh, I get it." She smacks her knee.

"No! Oh God, no!" I roll my eyes. "I need to take care of something."

"I'm just messing with you. Go get her." She winks.

"What?"

"Ellie." She points toward the basement level where the stage is. "You'd better hurry. She is only playing a couple songs before tonight's headliner."

"Jen..." I question on what I'm about to do. I left that night for a reason. I've been there, done that before.

"Don't think, Lee. Just go after her," she says before turning to walk away.

Spinning around, I take the steps as fast as I can without drawing attention to myself. They take security around this place seriously, especially with all the pop-in celebrities who stop by so they can go out without all the hassle.

"How's it going tonight? I heard we just had an engagement up in here!" Ellie hollers to the crowd, and they erupt in applause.

Pushing my way through the second level, I find the basement steps and take them as quickly as I had the ones before.

"For the final song, I'm going to slow it down a little and do a cover of one of my favorite artists. He's pretty *BAD* and has a way with singing about *Human Nature*." She laughs into the microphone as the crowd goes wild.

I can see her now; she takes a step back from mic as she strums the first chords. I can't help it. Something about her makes me want to just stand and watch.

She is absolutely stunning. Her dark hair, glowing shades of pink from the spotlights weaving through the crowd; her hazel eyes shining with the emotion the words can't say. She feels every. Single. Word. And makes her audience feel the same.

This is what drew me in, *her voice,* but her heart is what made me want to stay.

So complex and confused. Just from the short time I spent talking to her, I knew she was someone I wanted to spend more time with. And I'll be damned if I'm going to stay and chase this girl, risking everything for a chance, when I'm struggling to hold on to the only thing I've even known.

"Well, guys, that's it for me, but my girl who came all the way from Nashville, Tennessee, is here to bring a little country to the city life. Please welcome, the one, the only, Myles Davis."

Shit!

I was so wrapped up in her performance I'm still a hundred feet from her in a sold-out crowd. Working my way through the maze of people, I call out *excuse me, pardon* and *I'm so sorry* more times than I can count until I reach the stage, to only see her walking down the hall.

"Ellie! Wait up." I take off down the corridor and round the corner, skidding to a stop when I see the open back door and Ellie there talking to a man in a suit.

"Miss Hawthorne, your father has requested I pick you up."

Hawthorne?

"It's not necessary, thank you. I have my car." She tries to step past him, but he blocks her way.

"Mr. Hawthorne told me to not give you a choice. So, please do us both a favor and get in the back of the car." He lowers his head and his tone. "Please, Eloise. You know how your father gets."

"Malcolm, I was having a good night. High off life and this right here is bringing me down. A total buzzkill moment." Ellie takes a step forward and the driver moves aside, then follows behind.

I can't help myself. I already came this far. I have to watch her leave because chasing is no longer in the equation. Kicking the door open, I see the car driving away, nothing but fading taillights in the distance.

The chase over before it even began.

Ellie Thorne?

Eloise Hawthorne?

Neither one is the girl I thought I knew. Just a performer looking for her next show. Just like *her*.

Chapter Three
Ellie

"Miss Hawthorne?" I hear the fragile voice of Maggie, our housekeeper and former nanny, through the door.

"Come in." I sit up in bed, waiting for her to come in and bring me my hot tea. "You can set it down over there." I throw the covers off and pad over to the dresser to tie my hair up.

"I'm sorry, Eloise."

Here we go again. She is using the same sad tone Malcolm used on me.

"I didn't bring tea this morning. Your father is requesting your presence downstairs," she says, her eyes watering. "Eloise, my dear." Maggie takes a couple steps toward me, tucking a loose hair behind my ear. "He knows. He knows about the gigs. He knows you haven't been at school and you have been staying down the road with the Bowens." She shakes her head, before dropping her hand. "Sweetie, he knows you dropped out of school."

"Shit!"

"Maggie, I thought I told you to send Eloise down." My father's voice echoes down the hall.

"Eloise, sweetie, this is it. Now is your time. Prove them wrong.

Prove them all wrong," she whispers before she heads out. "She's coming!"

"The hell she is," he says angrily as he barges into the room. "Maggie, you may leave."

"Father, I-I can explain." I reach for my robe, slide it on and tie the belt, trying to occupy myself so I won't have to look my father in the eyes. "I couldn't do it and honestly why would you want me to keep on going, wasting your money like that."

"We made a deal. You finish this semester and we would discuss your future." He moves to stand in front of the window, pushing the curtains back and gazing outside. "One month. You only had one goddamn month. Was that so hard?"

"I was losing who I am. I was suffocating," I plead.

"Don't give me that shit. Now you are sounding like a spoiled little rich girl." He tries to yank the curtains closed but pulls the rod down instead. "Fuck!"

"Daddy—"

"Father," he spits out.

"Father, I know I told you I was going back to school after that night at Java Talk, but I couldn't. I really did try, but I couldn't."

"I'm not going to lose you to that life. I love you too much." He plops down on the bed, hands on his knees, a look of defeat present. It's a look I have rarely seen on his face.

"Daddy, you won't lose me. I promise." I move to stand beside him, placing my hand on his shoulder. "I just want to do what I *love*."

Raising his head, he just looks at me. The look of defeat gone, his fight back. "*Love?*" He takes his hand and flings mine away, standing up so quickly I almost fall back. "Little girl, this is reality and I'm afraid that your mom and I have catered to you for so long that you have become delusional."

"Daddy?"

"Eloise, this is your last warning. Address me as Father." He storms past me and into the walk-in closet, and comes back out with a small, carry-on suitcase. "You want to live this life? Make a living playing bars and coffee shops?" He throws the suitcase on the bed. "Everything you have *I* have provided it for you. So, I like to think I'm being pretty generous by letting you take this." He nods to the suitcase and continues. "Whatever you can fit in there, you can have."

"Father?"

"You want that life? No questions asked? You can have it, but you will *not* have our support." He turns and walks out.

"Father?" I run to the door and call after him. "This isn't what I want."

"You should have thought about that before you dropped out of school." He doesn't look back as he takes the stairs one by one. "You have thirty minutes."

Thirty minutes.

"You got this," I say to myself, wiping away the tears that threaten to spill over.

I'm suddenly thankful for those sleepless nights where I fell through the Facebook rabbit hole of video tutorials; I know how to pack for thirty days in a tiny carry-on.

Looking down at my phone, I mentally jot down a list.

Pack.

Shower.

Get dressed.

Get my guitar

Head to Nashville.

Five little tasks and not quite thirty minutes is all that's between me and making my dream a reality.

Bring it!

This isn't what I wanted or how I intended for this moment to go. I would have never dropped out of college if they would have opened their eyes and seen that I never belonged there in the first place.

I just wanted what everyone else wants: approval and support from two loving parents. What I received was a short leash and a list of demands and expectations.

Now I'm standing by the door, bags in hand, waiting for someone to come and stop me. They don't.

As I open the door, I blindly reach for my keys on the entry table.

"Are you looking for these?" My father's voice grabs my attention.

"If those are my keys, then yes," I snap as I turn around and see him standing with my keys dangling from his index finger.

"You mean my keys." He removes the Bob Dylan guitar pick my mother gave me with my guitar. A little secret we kept between us.

"Hey! That's mine." My eyes go wide at the thought of him just throwing the pick away. That little pick was the only support I have ever received from my mother, Anna Hawthorne. The one-time singer/songwriter. That is, until my father gave her an ultimatum.

"This little thing." He holds it up, examining it. "You can have it." He tosses it at my feet. "But these." He holds up the keys I have called mine since I graduated. "Are mine." He smirks as he tucks them in his perfectly pressed pants pocket.

"It was a graduation gift."

"My name is on the title." He strides toward me, hands still in his pockets while he looks me over, his silent judgment making me feel dirty. "You see…" He tilts his head to the side and crosses his arms, bringing a hand to his chin as he makes his statement. Because with my father, Nathaniel Joseph Hawthorne, every word is carefully thought out. "If you would have paid attention in your business classes, you would have learned all about assets, and how it's important to have them." He nods, trying to sell me on his statement, a move I have seen him do a hundred times in the courtroom.

My father is the most sought-after attorney in the Midwest. The problem with this whole screwed up little scene though is I'm not the judge nor the jury. I'm his freakin' daughter for crying out loud.

"You know what? I don't need the car. It's only a material possession, apparently one *you* own." I take a couple steps backward. The door is still open behind me. A few more feet and I'll be out of this prison for good.

"Nate, you can't just let her go out there with no means of transportation." My mother walks up behind him with a towel draped around her neck. Probably from morning yoga.

"If this is the life she wants to live, then let her do it." He wraps his arm around her and my mother leans, looking up at him.

"Nate," she pleads before she looks back to me.

"Mother, it's fine. I have a plan. Please don't worry about me." I turn to leave.

"And what's that exactly?" My father reaches past me and slams the door, blocking me in.

Dropping my bags, I begin to unleash everything I have ever wanted to say. The verbal vomit spews from my mouth.

"You know what? Contrary to what you think. I'm perfectly capable of making it on my own. I just haven't wanted to, but what did I want? My parents' support. Their love. Their acceptance." I look between my mother and father. "I wanted you to see the talent that Mom saw. You know, the same talent that she possesses."

"Eloise!" my mother gasps.

"You think you are so smart. You think you are capable of leaving here and making it on your *own*?" My dad reaches down, grabbing my designer handbag. "Let's see you try. It doesn't matter what talents you *think* you possess. You don't have what it takes to make this your business. To create a life." He opens my bag, taking out my wallet.

"Hey! That's mine." I reach for it, but he jerks away and takes out all my cards and the cash I had saved up.

"Correction. These cards were for your living expenses while you were in school." He counts the cash. "And this, I'm pretty sure, is from the bank account we provide for you."

"Nate." My mother is quickly beside him, placing a hand on his wrist, begging. "You can't send her out in this world without anything. She's *our* daughter."

At that, he throws his head back and laughs. "That is where you are mistaken, Anna. No daughter of mine would be so stupid."

"Nate!" She releases his wrist and comes to stand beside me.

Too late, Mother.

"Now we are getting somewhere. You see..." I can't stop what is about to come out of my mouth. A confession my mother entrusted to me. I know the truth, but I'm not sure if he does. "Maybe I'm not your daughter and that is what scares you. Keeping me locked up so you won't have to face the reality of your past." I walk over and pluck a couple hundred-dollar bills from his hand. "You can have the car and you can have the money because I don't want anything that has to do with you." I hold up the cash as I grab my things with the other hand. "And *this* is *mine*, from doing what I love. What I was *born* to do. No thanks to you!"

I storm out of the house, tears streaming down my face. My mother screams after me, but my father holds her back. In this moment, I should be worried about where I'm going to go or what I'm going to do. Instead I hold my head high because I know, in my heart of hearts, that I was born to be heard and today, I raised my voice!

This is only the beginning of Ellie Thorne!

Chapter Four
Ellie

Vision—blurred. Feet—tired. This isn't exactly how I imagined my grand exit, but it will have to do. I walk along the sidewalk, admiring the pristine lawns, in a neighborhood where the upkeep for landscaping is more than most families pay for their house. Kind of ridiculous if you ask me.

I pass house after house. Neighbors are staring, dogs are growling, and I have no idea what I'm going to do. With each block I leave behind, fear begins to creep in. The past month I have stayed with the Bowens. Actually, I was rooming with Rain, one of my closest friends, in her parents' pool house without their permission.

Her father inherited a small fortune from his father, but instead of just living a comfortable life, he decided to invest all his money in small Internet companies which just so happened to explode, making the man billions of dollars. Afterward, Jerry and Cheryl became Big Jer & Cher, quit their jobs, and became self-proclaimed hippies.

Everything seemed to be going fine at the Bowens' until I ran into Big Jer while he was tending to his organic herbs. I kept my head down and pretended I was just visiting, but he must have caught on and let the cat out of the bag when my mother went for one of her daily runs, causing this series of events to unfold.

Lucky me.

It crosses my mind to ask one of the neighbors for a ride to the bus stop and take the first bus out to Nashville, but what's the point? I don't even have my guitar. I left it in the back of Malcolm's car, just in case my dad was in one of his moods.

Besides not having a guitar, my phone had all my contacts. I had everything stored on my cell. Even a few songs I wrote while waiting in line, or at the coffee shop. If I had an idea, I jotted it down in my journal or on my phone. Now, I literally have nothing but two hundred dollars to my name and thirty days' worth of clothes.

With my feet screaming for me to stop, I set everything down and take a rest on top of the suitcase, looking forward, never looking back. I may not know *where* I'm going, but...

"Is that?" I stand, hearing a loud, familiar noise coming from around the corner.

It is!

Picking up my belongings, I wave frantically at the beat-up Honda Accord that is coming down the road. Bass pumping, windows down and the girl behind the wheel singing at the top of her lungs without a care in the world.

"Raaaaain!" I shout as she drives right past. "Raaaaain!" I scream again, causing a few homeowners to peer out their windows and Rain to slow to a stop, put the car in park and throw open her door.

"El, streetwalking doesn't suit you." She begins to walk toward me as I notice her car starting to roll down the road.

"Rain!" I point. "Your car."

"Shit!" She quickly turns, running to dive into her car and put on the emergency brake. "That was a close one." She pushes herself up and out. "So, where were we?" Rain looks around and notices my suitcase. "Oh yeah, you hookin'!"

"Shut up! I need a ride." I pick up my things and walk her way.

"Why didn't you say something?" She waves me on. "Get in."

Rounding the car, I throw what little I have in the back and climb in the front.

"You going to tell me what's going on?" She starts up the old beater and puts it into gear.

"Father." I give her the only word she needs to fill her in.

Rain looks at me out of the corner of her eye. "For good?" she questions as she turns to mess with the gears again. "Dammit! It's stuck again."

"Emergency brake." I point out. "And yes. For good."

"Thanks." She releases it and steps on the gas. "You wanna stay with me?"

"I can't. This isn't like all the other times." I stick my hand out the rolled-down window and weave my hand through the air as I tell her what happened. "Phone, money, car...all of it—gone."

"You don't need it anyway." She does a U-turn at the next stop.

"Where you taking us?"

"We are going to get me a burger and you an apartment." She looks over to me and grins.

"Rain! Weren't you listening? I have literally two hundred-dollar bills to my name. That's it. Credit cards are gone."

"Don't you worry that pretty little face of yours." She reaches over and pinches my cheek.

"Stop!" I laugh, slapping her hand away. "I can't help but worry. You aren't sending me to a whore house. I want to sing for money, not turn tricks."

"Just trust me."

"All right."

"All right?" Rain reaches over to feel my forehead. "Are you sick? I mean the last time you trusted me, I turned your hair—"

"Oh! My! God! I completely forgot about that!" I cut her off. "Ummm…"

"Seriously, El. I can't believe I didn't think of this a couple weeks ago. This place is going to be perfect for you."

"I hope so."

I need it to be.

Lee

After last night, I needed an everyday routine to forget about the past month, to busy myself with work.

So when Drew, my boss and the owner of WilliamSon Construction, called me up to handle a situation at one of the sites, I jumped right on it. Especially since today is their family day.

After all. it's just me and Grans. If I wasn't helping her, I would be working in the garage on my latest project. It only made sense for me to go, especially since I'm trying to prove myself. Rumor has it now that Kyle and Nina are engaged he will want to put in less hours. Even, possibly, step down from management. I want this promotion and my bank account *needs* it.

Today will be good. It's mindless work, really. Now that the ground is finally drying out from the torrential downpours we have been having, the landscapers can come in and do what they need to do. But first, I have to move the equipment and all the leftover materials.

Easy, right?

Pulling into the site, I put the truck in park and grab my hardhat. After the site accident last year, I will never forget this baby again. Any one of us could have been in Drew's shoes and he is damn lucky he didn't lose more than just a few memories. He could have lost his life.

Securing the hat, I open the door and head to the back of the truck when I hear my phone ring.

Grans!

Running back to the driver's side, I reach in and swipe it to life without looking.

"Grans, what's wrong?" My voice is quick and nervous. My heart rate picks up when she doesn't respond. "Grans?" I shout.

"Lee?" Drew's voice seems unsure. "Is this you, man?"

Switching to speaker, I throw the phone in the seat and try to gather my nerves. With my hands on my knees, I try to slow my breathing.

"Yeah, it's me. I'm sorry, I thought..."

What *did* I think? That she was going through another episode? That she had an accident?

"Is everything okay with your Grans?" Drew sounds concerned.

"Yeah. She just had a small episode and..." I pause, worried I already said too much. I can't have him thinking my life is too complicated to take on more. "She's fine." I cut myself short.

"Well good. I have a proposition for you," Drew says, saving me from my worst fears.

"What's up?" I reply as I dig around the truck for my earpiece.

Got it!

Sliding it on, I grab the phone and switch it over to Bluetooth.

"Well, the girls have been watching this warrior show where they battle it out through various obstacles to see who can claim the title for top warrior." Drew exhales loudly. "And, well, I thought it would be cool to build a rock wall and surprise Andie and Reece with it tomorrow morning."

"Okay?"

"It's huge, Lee. It's in three pieces." He lets out a laugh. "And heavy as hell."

"So you need help?" Amused I cut to the chase. I'm glad to help out. Drew has always been good to me.

"Yeah, man. I would have asked Kyle, but they took off on vacation and won't be back for a couple weeks."

"No problem. I'll be there after I finish up here."

"Actually, can you come around nine? When all the kids are in bed. Like I said—surprise."

"Sure. Not a problem." I gather a few tools and head toward the house.

"Thanks, Lee, I owe you one."

"Just buy me a drink some time." I reach the garage where we have a few tools set up with our white board of projects. "Hey, Drew?"

"Yeah?"

"I just noticed that the board says the landscapers will be here Monday the tenth, but the tenth is actually today." I head to the table to go through a few files.

"Dammit. I wonder if Kyle switched the date." I can hear him tapping out a message over the phone. "Hey, look in the files, should be the green folder on the bottom."

"Found it." I shuffle through some papers. "Today. They will be here around five with the load and then be back at dawn tomorrow."

"Shit! It's coming back to me now. With Kyle preparing for the proposal, I just had too much going on."

"No problem." I try to reassure him, but looking down at my watch, I'm not so sure I can pull this off by myself. "I'll call Justin. He's home from college and needs more hours than the lumberyard can give him. If you are cool with doing the paperwork Monday and paying him OT for today, I'm sure he will be in."

This is the perfect opportunity to prove myself, to show Drew I'm capable of stepping in and taking charge.

"Make this happen, Lee. Whatever it takes," Drew orders. "And if you need me, call. We *have* to get this done to stay on schedule."

"Heard loud and clear. I got this." I search my phone for Justin's number. "Just enjoy your family.

"Give me an update in a few hours."

"Deal." I start to press end.

"Lee, thank you. Just know this is not going unnoticed." He hangs up.

A grin spreads across my face. "Yes!" I shout, pumping my fist in the air. I need to calm down and get a move on it, secure Justin before he commits to something else. That dude is resourceful as hell and refuses to sit still for a minute.

This is exactly what I needed, work to take my mind off all things Ellie. The girl who captivated me from the first pickup line is also the same girl who lied about who she *really* is. But why? What does she have to hide?

Why do you even care?

I shake my head back and forth to try to lose the lingering thoughts. "Get busy. Gain a promotion," I chant to myself.

I *need* this promotion and I refuse to let anyone, especially Ellie Thorne or Eloise Hawthorne or whoever the hell she is, distract me from that.

I'm tired of chasing lies. Today, I'm fighting for my truth. For the one person who has always been there. And I refuse to let *her* down.

Chapter Five

Ellie

"Seriously, Rain?" I shout, following behind her, but this girl is on a mission and isn't stopping for anyone.

"Listen." She turns around and walks backward. "When have I ever let you down?" She holds out a finger, waiting for me to name them off, but truth be told, this girl says what she means and means what she says. I always know where I stand and if Rain says she is going to do something, she will do it.

"Nothing?" She turns around and heads toward the bar, calling over her shoulder, "That's what I thought. Now let's get some meat!"

I can't help but throw my head back in laughter. Since her parents turned hippy-ish, Rain has struggled to live the vegan lifestyle her parents insist she have. In middle school, she would come over and eat our pantry empty. Once Maggie caught on, she would pack her a two-week survival kit to last until the next visit. No questions asked, just a silent exchange before Rain went back home.

Pulling out a stool, I settle in and signal to the bartender to get me a menu.

"No need, my friend." Rain pushes my hand back down. "Two in-out burgers, double order of fries with cheese and bacon," she calls to the blonde.

"What if I didn't want a burger?" I raise an eyebrow.

"I'm going to pretend you didn't just say that." She leans over and begins to whisper, "These burgers are amazing. A half-pound of lean buffalo meat, stuffed with cheese, bacon, onions and did I say bacon? Because it has bacon."

"So you ordered me a bacon cheeseburger."

Rain gasps. Holding a hand over her mouth, she pretends to be insulted. "Not just a cheeseburger. This is better than that. Hell, it's better than..." She closes her eyes and wipes her mouth. "Sex. El, it's the perfect beef orgasm."

"Why do I feel so dirty right now?" I lean away from her. "I need to take a shower after all that—" I stop mid-sentence. Realization sets in, once again.

Shower.

I can't even take a shower if I want to. I'm freaking homeless. Bound to live on the streets, playing for food. Wait! I can't even do that. My guitar is stuck in the back of a town car at my parent's house.

"I'm going to keep talking dirty." She leans into me and continues. "Because I'm getting you an apartment, with a shower." She turns and looks me in the eyes. "Today."

"How? I don't even have the money to pay for a deposit, let alone first month's rent." I'm on the verge of tears. I know Rain has something up her sleeve, but after the morning I had, thinking positive is becoming harder and harder to do.

"Hey, look!" Rain sits up straight. "Our food!" She does a little shimmy in her seat.

"I'm not that hungry." I hunch over.

"Jake, these look delicious!" Rain proclaims as she claps, bouncing up and down in her seat.

"Damn, Bow." The guy, whom I presume is Jake, chuckles at Rain. "I don't think I have ever met someone who enjoys food as much as you." He sets our plates down in front of us.

Turning to look at Rain I mouth "Bow?" questioning this little nickname he has given her. Who is this Jake and how does she know him?

Rolling her eyes. "Ellie, meet Jake Morgan, the new manager of Spotlight. Also, the brother of Jordan, my ex."

"Don't hold it against me." Jake holds up both hands.

"Ohhhhh! I can kind of see it now." I examine Jake from head to toe. Dark hair, light eyes and a smile that is bound to knock your panties off. "I'm Ellie—"

"Thorne. You know, the singer from last night," Rain cuts in.

"I thought you looked familiar." He takes my hand and gives it a shake. "Nice to meet you."

"You too." I give his hand a little squeeze before letting go.

"I'll let you guys finish up here and when you are done, just holler at Cindy." He points to the blonde at the other end of the bar. "And she will come and get me, and I'll take you upstairs."

I glance over at Rain, wondering what he's talking about.

"I haven't told her yet." Rain picks up her glass, takes the straw into her mouth and drains her drink, then sets it back down and looks at me. "Surprise! You are going to live at Spotlight!" She holds out her arms. "You're welcome. Now eat." She picks her burger back up, taking a huge bite for such a tiny mouth.

"In a club?" I look between Jake and Rain. "Here?"

Rolling her eyes, she covers her mouth with one hand as she speaks through a mouthful of food. "No, El, in the apartment upstairs."

"Jake, I'm sorry, apparently my friend has been getting into her parents' herb garden, if you know what I mean. I can't afford an apartment right now."

"Ellie." Jake takes a step closer. "Bow texted me on the way over here. I don't know all the details and I'm sure we can work something out later, but the apartment is yours if you want it. For however long you need it."

"Really?" The hope begins to build inside me.

"Yes, really." He slaps the top of the bar. "Eat now, negotiations later." He smiles, then walks off.

"Did this just really happen?" I swivel to face Rain. "I have a place to stay?"

"I told you I would take care of this."

"I'm not going to be homeless?"

"Ellie, we could have snuck you into the pool house, but this?" She swirls her finger in the air. "This was meant to happen. I was in here the other day, getting my protein fix, when I overheard Jake talking to someone about the apartment."

"I didn't even know there was apartments up there," I interrupt.

"I know! Neither did I, but apparently there are two and now one of them is yours."

"I'm not going to have to sleep with him, am I?" Dread starts to fill the pit of my stomach. Jake isn't a bad looking guy, but I do have some morals.

"Well, he's nothing like his brother—"

"OH MY GOD, you didn't whore me out for a room." I raise my voice forgetting there are people surrounding me. The blonde turns, giving me a look.

"You should see the look on your face." She attempts to get the last drop from her empty glass before standing. "You done?" She motions to my food.

"Yeah. I'm just not feeling good."

"Cindy, can we get a to-go box and the check please?" Rain picks up her purse and lays down the tip.

"It's on Jake," Cindy says as she walks toward us, grabbing a box on her way. "I'll tell him you are ready."

I watch Cindy round the corner before I speak up. "So, what exactly is the exchange? I mean, no one is going to let me stay here for free."

"I'm not sure yet, but I trust Jake." She pulls me up and into a hug. "El, please don't worry," she whispers into my hair. "I know it's scary, but you wanted this."

"I know." My words are barely a whisper.

"You're *free*. Time to live your dreams." Rain lets go of me. "Time to do you, babe." She reaches up, brushing a lone tear from my cheek.

"You're right! Time to do me." I smile weakly.

"Yeah, you will!" She winks. "Now, let's go see what a fresh start looks like."

"I like the sound of that."

"Now don't get your hopes up," Jake warns us as we follow him upstairs. "It's not much, but I think it'll work for you." He unlocks the door.

"Seriously Jake, if it has a bed, bathroom and coffee pot, I'm good." I bounce from foot to foot, nervous that I'm going to walk through these doors and see someplace I can call home, only for him to whip out a contract, the catch. *Losing it all.*

"I think we can do a little bit better than that." He wiggles the knob. "If we can get this damn knob to turn," Jake huffs out as he pulls the key out and tries again.

"Lift up on the knob and push in," a man says as he comes around the corner, heading for the apartment across the hall. "I thought that apartment was for the talent?" He heads in, slamming the door behind him.

"That's Shapiro." Jake pushes up and in. "Well look at that." He swings the door wide for us to walk through. "Feel free to look around, but I do need an answer by the end of today."

Rain pushes through, but I stand still, frozen. I need this to work out, but what if it doesn't? What if I walk in there and it's a shithole or, worse, what if I love it and I can only stay if I agree to give him my left kidney or part of a lung or some weird crap like that.

"Seriously, El." I can almost hear Rain's eyes roll. "Get your ass in here." She turns around and grabs me by the elbow. "You are going to love it!" She turns me toward her and grips my shoulders, looking me straight in the eyes. "Trust a little." She forces me to look.

My eyes dart from the kitchen to the living room to the bed to the bathroom and repeat. How can something this nice be compacted into such a small area?

"This is…" I turn around in a circle, making sure I don't miss anything. "I mean, it's everything." It's a small loft, but it has it all. Fully equipped kitchen, island with seating, leather loveseat and flat screen TV.

"El, this is so cool! Looks like a bachelor pad." Rain goes to stand by Jake. "Let's cut to the chase and tell us exactly what it is you need."

"Well, once your friend here texted me who she was bringing by, I did my research and apparently we had you on our list to contact for a weekly gig." Jake pulls a rolled-up sheet of paper from his back pocket.

"I'll take it!" I blurt out.

"Well, there's more. We need a bartender-slash-waitress," he says as he closes the distance between us, handing me the paper. "Basically, if you work these hours, and play this many times a week, you can stay here for free."

"That's awesome, but she will have no money for food and her other bills." Rain chimes in as I smooth out the paper and read over the terms.

"You will get to keep all tips. During the afternoon rush that could be around a couple hundred dollars, but I think we could find a spot for you one night a week. I want to say they make…" His lips purse while he thinks, keeping me on edge. "An average of about four hundred a night."

"I'll take it!" My voice comes out as a shout as I wave the paper in the air. "Where do I sign?"

"Yes! Yes! Yes!" Rain jumps her way over to me, causing me to do the same. The room is filled with squeals and shouts. "Thanks Jake!" She jumps right into his arms.

"No problem, Bow." He sets her back down. "I just need to know how long you plan on staying."

Staying?

I haven't really thought about it. If I would have had the money, I would have left today. "I'm not sure."

"We can leave it open-ended. Just make sure if you decide to leave us for bigger and better things, you give us the courtesy of a two-week notice."

"That I can do!" I set the paper down on the island and dig through my purse for a pen.

Eloise Hawthorne.

My signature is a sad reminder of who I was. But I'll have a new life here, the start of who I'm about to become.

"Can she move in today?" Rain stands there chomping her gum as she types out a text, her face scrunching up. "Did you tell your brother I was here?"

"Sure. You can keep those." He points to the keys on the island. "I'll just need this." Jake swoops up the paper. "And Rain, I think we need to talk."

"Fine." She pulls me in for a hug. "I'm so happy for you! This is exactly what you needed and I'm so proud of you for going after your dream. Don't ever give up." She gives me a tight squeeze before letting go. "I'm just going to grab your bag out of the car."

"Thank you for everything." I begin to tear up as I follow them out. "I don't know what I would have done if you didn't show up today."

Waving me off as they leave, Rain turns around. "You would have walked your ass into town and found a way to Nashville." She wags her finger at me. "There is no doubt in my mind about that. You, my friend, are destined to be someone, but it's up to you to find out who." She turns back around and heads down the hall, leaving me alone in my new apartment.

My apartment.

Exhaling a breath I didn't know I was holding, I walk around the room, touching everything within reach. This is mine. I live here. *Alone.* All my life I have lived with someone. My parents, in a dorm, friend's house in Nashville, Rain's. But today, I have a place. *Mine.*

A perfect start to a new beginning.

Chapter Six

Lee

Why?

It's a question I ask myself daily. How can someone with so much more life to live forget how to live it?

Forget her past?

Forget me?

I thought I had more time to figure things out. To get the resources together to place her in a home that would be able to care for her. Instead of listening to the doctor, I held on to hope.

I thought if the good moments outweighed the bad, we were fine. We would go days, sometimes months, without having an episode, making it easy to wait one more day.

Then one day became two, and two became a month, and a month became three years.

Three years since Grans had been diagnosed and we were surviving.

Until now.

In the beginning I didn't understand. I thought if we had a neighbor check in on her daily, we would be fine

I was wrong.

I thought if I held on to the good moments and forgot the bad, that we could prepare not only mentally, but financially. I wasn't ready to make the arrangements that I'm being informed I need to make. Now, I pull into the only home I have ever known to a driveway of first responders.

"Dammit!" I shout, slamming my palm against the steering wheel.

They're here because of *me*. Because of my neglect. I assumed that she would be with me forever.

I need her to be.

Coming to a stop, I put my truck in park and hop out. I'm running to the house when I hear Katie, a retired teacher and our neighbor, shout. "Lee! Over here!"

I jog over to the ambulance where Katie is sitting in back, holding Grans' hand as they check her out. I can't help but worry. Will she know me?

When she was first diagnosed, I did a little bit of research before I slammed my laptop shut and pushed it to the back of my mind. Grans is strong, alert and young. There is no way this will happen to her.

But it has.

Is there a way I could have prolonged this if I dug deeper? Maybe I could have found a research study to put her in, or a clinical trial? By ignoring it, did I make it come faster? Is this my fault?

"Grans?" I whisper her name, knowing she can't hear me.

"Lee, she's fine." Katie reaches with her other hand to take mine and continues in her "teacher voice." "She was boiling chicken to make dumplings, then laid down for a nap."

"Are you Lee Scott?" The fire chief walks up to me, notepad in hand.

"Yes, sir."

"Your neighbor here," he tilts his head in Katie's direction, "filled me in on your grandmother's situation."

"How bad is it?" I interrupt, asking him a loaded question.

"Well, she's lucky you had Katie here checking in. Apparently when she went to boil the chicken she failed to fill the pot with water, causing the chicken to eventually catch fire. Katie was able to get your grandmother, who was pretty disoriented, out of the house before she called nine-one-one and went back in with an extinguisher."

"Katie?" I look up and examine her face, giving her hand a squeeze. I need for her to tell me Grans was just tired, that she didn't forget what she was doing or where she was at.

"I don't know, Lee," Katie responds. "But she fell when I was trying to get her out of the house and hit her head on the corner of the nightstand."

"Oh God." I throw my head back, closing my eyes, inhaling the evening air. I try to push back the fear of what could have happened.

"Son, this is not your fault. It was one hundred percent accidental." The fire chief clasps my shoulder. "You have maybe a couple thousand dollars in smoke and fire damages, but lives weren't lost. You *got* to hold on to that."

"Thank you, sir." I release Katie's hand and extend it to the chief. "For all your help."

"It's what we're here for." He gives me a firm shake and heads back to his crew.

"Mr. Scott?" the EMT calls out, drawing my attention back to Grans.

"How is she?"

"Honestly, she gave us a hard time when we first got here, but once we got the IV in she relaxed and fell asleep."

"I'm NOT asleep." Grans pops open an eye. "I was simply resting my eyes."

"Mrs. Scott, in other words, passed out when she saw the needle, but given the fall, we want to have her checked out." The EMT is smirking at Grams.

"The hell if you are!" she shouts, sitting up.

"Grans, please lay back down," I plead.

"Whoa." Gran begins to lower herself back down. "Lee, you really shouldn't spin around like that."

"I'm not."

"Okay, twirling. Why are you twirling?" She chuckles.

"I'm not twirling either." I'm irritated.

"Maybe you should." She taps her IV. "Hit me big boy."

"You gave her morphine?" I pull myself up into the truck then help Katie get down.

"No, but I told her I was since that was the only way she was going to allow me to get close with a needle. She needed fluids," he says defensively.

"I live with her. Trust me, I get it." I let out a much-needed laugh.

"We are going to take her to the hospital to get her head checked out. You riding along?" He jumps out, and his partner climbs in.

"Yeah." I holler out to Katie, "You around later?"

"Whatever you need, Lee. You got my number. Call and I'll come up." Katie gives me a weak smile.

"Wait! I need Biscuit!" Grans tries to push herself up, but the EMT beside me settles her down.

"We can get you something to eat when we get there. After the doctor checks you over." He winks.

But I know she's not talking about food. Biscuit was the Yorkshire Terrier my grandfather gave her. Her *baby*. The problem? He died two years ago.

"Grans, Biscuit..." I swallow the word I dread to say. "Died."

"Presley Aaron Scott!" She uses my full name as a curse. The name I have tried for so long to forget. "I may be getting old, but I'm not senile."

"But you asked for—"

"My pillow?" She stares at me wide-eyed like I'm the idiot, and right now, I feel like one. "The one with a picture of Biscuit on it." She rolls her eyes at me, something she has been doing more frequently. "Don't tell me you thought..." She examines my face. "Presley, you're telling your grans that you thought..." She shakes her head. "You did! I just need it to sleep. The pillow. Not my dead dog."

Thank God.

Each time she forgets something, I cringe knowing what's to come.

Obsession.

Is it normal? Is it the disease? Is it my imagination?

"Presley? Your grans needs Biscuit," she begs.

"Guys, can you give me two minutes? This pillow...it's

sentimental," I plead.

"Sure thing," they both agree.

Jumping down from the ambulance, I hurry into the house. On the way back my phone begins to vibrate in my back pocket. I pull it out and see it's Drew.

Crap!

So much for the promotion. Between me and Justin we had the site almost prepared for the landscapers, but then I got the call from Katie about the fire.

I left Justin with strict orders and tried to call Drew, but he didn't answer. I had no choice but to leave him a quick voicemail about what is going on, hoping that he understood.

Being on the phone with Drew while riding in back of an ambulance with Grans…what to do? It's a no-brainer. After sending him to voicemail, I shoot him a quick text saying that everyone is fine, and I'll fill him in tomorrow.

This is beyond my control. If I lose a promotion or hell, even my job, over this, then I do. Reaching the truck, I hop up and the EMT shuts the doors one at a time.

"Is this what prison feels like?" Grans wonders.

"I wouldn't know."

"How about you?" She nods to the EMT sitting next to me. "You have all those markings all over your body. You been to the slammer?"

"Grans!" I reprimand.

"What? I was watching this show—"

"Forgive her." I cut Grans off before she can tell us about some show she saw on the ID Channel.

"I guess you really should have given me morphine." She winks to the poor guy. "That's it!" Her eyes light. "You were a drug dealer or wait, maybe you were a supplier? They all have those things." She points to his arm.

"Apparently, I'm your drug dealer." He winks, making Grans smile.

"Not yet." She winks back.

"Am I in the twilight zone?" I bring my hands up and rub my face, trying anything to rid myself of the memories of today. I feel the phone vibrate and when I pull it from my pocket I see I have a text from Drew.

Drew: No worries. Family first.

Four words is all it takes to ease my mind. I still have a job. Whether or not I get the promotion…I can't let that bother me. Right now, all my free time will be going to finding a place for Grans when the time comes.

I'm going to check into home health care. What happened today will not happen again.

Losing more time with Grans is not an option.

Chapter Seven
Ellie

As I reach my arms above my head and stretch my legs, a yawn escapes—a reflection of the morning that came too soon.

Before, I would have closed my eyes, snoozed the alarm and tested the limits of punctuality. But today, I'm excited. You would think after a couple of weeks of the same routine that it would get old—the late nights and early mornings—but it doesn't.

Even though this is a life I was forced into, it was *my* choice that led to the circumstances. *No regrets.*

Or so I tell myself. I guess I would be lying if I were to say it didn't bother me how the events unfolded. I tried to raise my voice so I could be heard, but my wants fell upon deaf ears. Especially my father's. My mom, she loved my father and even though she tried to support and fight for me as much as she could, when it came down to it, she chose him. She would always choose him.

Throwing my legs over the side of the bed, I welcome the coldness of the ceramic floor as I pad to the kitchen. Heating the kettle of water causes me to miss the mornings I spent at the house. Maggie, every morning, would bring up a tray filled with pastries, fruit and tea for two.

To some this would look like I had S.R.G.S., otherwise known as spoiled rich girl syndrome, but not so. Maggie was more than a housekeeper. She was my nanny, like a second mother. Those mornings, she brought me tea, but I fixed her one as well.

We would lounge around for an hour or two depending on her day's schedule, talking about anything and everything. She gave me what I craved from my parents. *Support.* Maggie not only loves me, she cares about my passion for music. Accepts me for who I am.

I miss her.

While I wait for the water to heat, I head over to the sitting area and pull out my guitar.

This, my guitar—the feel of the neck in my hand, the back of the body against mine—is my security blanket. *Home.* And thanks to Maggie, I have it back. She didn't know where to find me, but she knew where I hung out and Java Talk was one of those places. Thankfully, Jen was working when Maggie took my guitar there and made sure it ended up back in my hands.

Glancing out the window, I strum the chords, trying out a new melody, contemplating the everyday that awaits me outside these doors. Doors I have refused to open.

I know I should venture out and find other gigs, contact a few friends in the business, but right now I like the little secluded world I live in. Opening the doors opens *me* up to disappointment, and who needs that?

I switch gears and start playing an old favorite. Humming along to the tune brings me back to the night at Java Talk. Lee, standing there smiling, eyes shining, watching my every move and then, I played this song and he left. As soon as he walked into my life, he ran back out.

He had my name. Well, my stage name, but still. He could have found me. Then again, I have his.

Hello, pot—kettle?

Speaking of which, mine is screaming at me to get along with my day.

Fix tea.

Shower.

Dress.

Work.

Nap.

Play.

Sleep.

This is what my life has become. It doesn't define who I am tomorrow, but it does define who I am today and I'm okay with that.

Always running late. Well, technically, I'm not late, but I wouldn't call it early either. Grabbing my purse, I run out the door and right into another.

"Shit!" I drop my purse, all of its contents scattering at my feet. When I see the door, it turns out not to be a door at all, but a young woman, maybe around my age or so. She just stands there with a deer in headlights look. Frozen.

"I'm so sorry. I was in a hurry and wasn't paying attention," I apologize, yet she continues staring. *Silent.*

"Do you live across the hall?"

Nothing.

"Well, I just moved in a couple weeks ago." I motion behind me with my thumb. "I'm surprised we haven't run into each other before, but then again, I have weird hours." I continue to talk, unsure what to say but the silence is awkward.

Blink.

Sticking out my hand, I introduce myself. "I'm Ellie."

She looks down at my outreached hand, then looks me in the eyes and blinks a few more times before she speaks. "Hey," she whispers, giving me a quick wave before she turns on her heel and locks herself in her apartment.

Throwing my purse over my shoulder, I hurry down the three flights of stairs and into the breakroom, stuffing my purse into my locker.

"There you are!" Cindy exclaims, startling me. She's holding on to the doorframe as she peeks her head in. "Someone is here to see you."

Clutching my chest, I let out a rush of air. "You scared the hell out of me."

"Sorry. We are slammed out there. It's like everyone showed up at once." She nonchalantly points out that I'm late.

"I'm so sorry. I literally ran into my neighbor, or I think that's who she is." I smooth out my little black dress before I tie my Spotlight apron around my waist.

Cindy scrunches her brow. "Shapiro?"

"No, some girl." I head toward the door to follow Cindy out. "She just stared at me. Barely spoke."

"Ohhhh! Yeah, I'm not sure who she is. None of us are." We round the corner to the bar when she whispers, "And when we ask, Shapiro quickly shuts us down."

"Interesting."

"Excuse me, Miss?" A familiar voice calls down from the opposite end of the bar. "I need to get the biggest steak you have." Rain grins from ear to ear, holding her hands out wide. "HUGE."

Reaching below the counter, I grab a menu and call back. "Miss, I'm afraid to break the news to you, but steak is only served on the dinner menu. May I suggest a bean burger?" I watch her face as her outstretched arms cross.

"Very funny, El."

Slapping the menu on the counter, I turn to fill a couple glasses when Cindy comes up beside me, wiping off her hands.

"I need you to take a table." She busies herself by beginning to fix a few drinks. "There is this guy who I had a quick thing with. It's over and now he's engaged." I slowly begin to turn around, when Cindy's hand flies out to stop me. "Don't turn around he will know I'm talking about him."

Taking a side-step closer to her, I look at the reflection in the mirror.

"Kyle was just..." She turns toward me, leaning her hip against the counter. "A mistake."

"Kyle?" Who is Cindy talking about? I scan the crowd and my eyes fall on the table I think she means.

I can't believe it. Spinning around, I turn to see it for myself. It's him. He's here.

Lee.

Lee

Ellie. She's here.

Someone of her talent doesn't stay put, they pass through. But she's here. In Spotlight. Standing just a few feet away. Her hazel eyes meet mine.

I'm not sure what I'm feeling. It was just one night of conversation more than a month ago. Nothing more, nothing less.

"Lee?" Kyle speaks up, pulling my attention back to him.

"Uh, yeah." I turn to face him, clearing my throat.

"Let's talk business. I've talked to Drew and we both feel..." He clasps his hands together. "Oh look! Time to order. Hope you know what you want."

"I hear the burgers are—" I turn to see Ellie walking up, taking all the words from my mouth.

Ellie is absolutely breathtaking. Her hair, pulled back, exposes her slender neck. A neck I now envision biting.

Where is this coming from?

"Hi. My name is Ellie and I'll be your server today." She plasters a fake smile across her face as she sets our drinks down.

I'm not sure what comes over me, but something she said that night at Java Talk gives me an idea. Holding out my hand, I say, "I'm

Lee. It's a pleasure to meet you."

Cocking her head to the side, her smile now genuine, she takes my offered hand, giving it one hell of a squeeze. One I'm almost sure is meant to be as painful as it is. "Nice to meet you."

"Okay then!" Kyle interrupts, handing the menus over the table to Ellie. "We both will have the burger with onion rings and two Coors Lights."

"Got it!" She gives me a once over before turning around and leaving.

"You are so in trouble." Kyle shakes his head. "How long?"

"How long?" I echo, unsure of what he's getting at.

"How long have you had a thing for her?" he asks.

"I don't know her," I lie.

Kyle leans back and cocks an eyebrow.

"Okay. I barely know her," I admit.

"I'm not buying it."

"Fine." I continue my confession. "I met her a little over a month ago. We talked, it was nice and then I left."

"You left?"

"I left."

"I think there is more you're not telling me, but that is neither here nor there." Kyle reaches into a folder and pulls out some papers.

"Obviously, you don't want to talk about it and I respect that, so let's get down to business."

"I'm all ears." I sit back and wait for what I hope is a proposal that will solve all my problems.

"Drew filled me in on your grandmother."

"I promise, she won't be a problem. I have a home nurse coming for part of the day and the other I have neighbors checking in," I interrupt, needing to explain myself.

Shutting the folder, Kyle leans over the table. "Lee, I've been in your shoes. I know the desperation you are feeling. I'm not here to scold you for putting your family first. I want to help."

"Boss, I'm not looking for a handout. I just want a chance to prove myself," I reply.

"First off, you're going to have to cut out the "boss" comments. Especially since you are going to be one yourself." He sits back in his chair, watching my reaction.

I did it!

"Are you saying what I think you are saying?" I pick up my water, draining the glass.

"Not exactly."

There it is. Reality crashing down front and center. Crushing all my plans.

"Lee, I want to train you to take over my position at WilliamSon Construction. Drew and I both feel you are the only person with the leadership skills, drive and determination that could fulfill the job."

"Thank you, Boss."

"Kyle or Lewis, but 'boss' has to go," he says, smiling over my head. "Here comes your girl."

"Huh?"

"Two Coors Lights." Ellie sets the long necks in front of us. "Your burgers will be out shortly." She looks between the two of us. "Anything else?" She stands there, tugging on the tie of her apron.

"I think we're good. Thanks." Kyle picks up the beer, taking a long pull while Ellie walks off. "You drinking?"

"I'm on the clock." I push the beer away. "Not a good idea."

"We are ahead of schedule. I sent the crew home," he responds, pushing the beer back toward me.

"Well, in that case." I hold out my bottle. "Cheers."

"To new beginnings." Kyle clinks my bottle.

"New beginnings. I like that," I confess, letting my eyes roam the crowd for the girl who has been crossing my mind since the moment our gazes locked.

"Instead of sitting there, waiting for her to come to you, why don't you go after her?" Kyle breaks the silence.

"I'm going to use the restroom." I stand, scooting the chair back.

"Riiiiight." Kyle winks.

"Thanks for the advice."

I zigzag in between the tables on my way to the bar. She's disappeared, but a girl at the end of the bar hollers out, "She went to the restroom."

Perfect.

Nodding my thanks, I hurry down the hall and wait against the wall. I'm not sure what I'm going to say or do, but this is my one chance to make this right.

"I play tonight, actually. You should come," Ellie says to the woman she follows out, ignoring my presence.

"I think I will. Thank you." The woman brushes up against the wall trying to cut through, knocking a picture down. "Oh no." She bends to pick it up.

"I got it." Ellie waves her off. "You wouldn't believe how many times someone has knocked this thing down. I'm about to bolt it to the wall," she says to put the lady at ease.

I push myself off the wall as Ellie bends down to pick up the picture.

She stands and I rush up behind her and whisper, "Are you tired?" I come to a halt as I run into her. Quickly steadying her with my hands, I lean in, my lips brushing her ear. "Because you have been running through my mind all afternoon."

She whips around, smiling. "Well, well, well."

"How was that? Did it work?"

"I could do better." She spins on her heel to leave.

"Oh no you don't." I reach for her arm, turning her back around. "Have coffee with me."

"I play tonight."

"Okay then, tomorrow?" I counter. I'm not leaving here until she says yes.

"No, I meant I play tonight so how about in a couple hours." Her face begins to show worry. "That is, if you promise not to run off this time."

I hate that I did that to her, put doubt in her mind, but I couldn't stay knowing she would eventually leave.

"Scout's honor." I hold my fingers up, switching between two and three, not really sure what I'm doing.

"You weren't a Scout, were you?" She pushes my arm away. Our fingers brush against each other and just for a second, I hold on to her fingertips, letting them slowly slip away.

"Nope."

"Cute. How about I meet you there in, say, three hours?" Ellie suggests.

"Perfect. It's a date," I answer, before my brain can process what girly things it's saying.

"A date." She shakes her head. "You're cute." She turns her attention to someone shouting her name. "I better go. I think your food is up," she says as she walks away, leaving me standing here like the happiest idiot alive.

Maybe Kyle is right. With each door closing a new one opens.

To new beginnings.

Chapter Eight
Ellie

"What is your deal? Ever since that guy left you have been all sunshine, rainbows and that whipped cream crap in the middle of those tasty little snack cakes." Rain calls me out on my sudden mood change.

I try my best to avoid her interrogation. "I have no clue what you are talking about."

"Just give me his name and stats if you have them," she persists.

I give in. "Lee Scott, he's twenty-four, works in construction, and lives with his grandmother, whom he calls Grans." I stop there, trying to recall what else I know, but the rest seems too personal to share with Rain.

"Sweet. He's young, hot and can work with his hands." She snorts. "That's doable." She smacks her hand against the bar. "Get it? Doable?"

"Yeah, you perv." I point my finger in her direction. "I swear you are a horny thirteen- year-old boy, trapped in a twenty-something's body."

"And that's a bad thing?" She waggles her brows at me.

"You are something else." I shake my head and try to focus on work. One more hour is all that's separating me from a night of what-ifs. What if he would have stayed? What if he would have asked me out again?

Shit!

I slap my forehead. "I'm so stupid."

I've been so caught up in my own little world for the past two weeks that I haven't even realized that I don't have a car.

"What?" Rain stands like she is about to come around the bar.

"Car." I throw my hands up. "I told Lee I would meet him at Java Talk and that is all the way across town."

"Ohhhhh!" She settles back down.

"Can I borrow yours?" I fold my hands together and begin to plead with my friend. If I can't borrow it, she will surely drop me off and Lee can bring me back and if he doesn't, then obviously there won't be a date number two.

"Actually, I have to head home in five minutes. Can you leave now and I'll just drop you off on the way?"

"I have to help Cindy clean up before the next shift arrives." I sigh, ready to just throw in the towel. "Where you going?"

"Big Jer and Cher asked if I could come home to prepare for tonight's festivities." Rain rolls her eyes. "It's like a huge deal to them. Tonight the moon is supposed to be at its fullest. Like some kind of harvest moon, or maybe it's a blue one. Hell, I don't know, but it's a big ball of glowing shit in the sky. So they insist on feasting on a meal full of superfoods that help with fertility then head out to kneel in front of the garden of gods and pray to the man on the moon to someday give me a child," she rambles.

"Umm, am I the only one who sees an issue with this?" I throw my head back, not being able to contain it anymore. Some of the things the Bowens do are downright crazy.

"I know! I've been living a life feasting on cows and snack cakes. If this is what it takes to have a family, I'm screwed." She tilts her cup in my direction. "Can I get a cherry coke to go? Half the ice, double the cherries?"

As much as she claims to be different, there are times where I wonder how much of an influence her parents' lifestyle has on her.

"Dude, you aren't even married." I reach for a cup and begin layering cherries and ice, the way Rain likes it.

"Now, Eloise Hawthorne." She puts her hands on her hips. "I know your parents taught you the birds and the bees. You don't' have to be married to get knocked up."

Narrowing my eyes, I fill her cup, topping it off with a few more cherries. "Yes, Rain. I know where babies come from, but come on now—"

"You should see your face. Lord, El, I know this shit is crazy. My parents have lost their ever-loving minds, but they are still my parents and if me eating from our magical garden outside makes them happy, then hell, I'll do it." She laughs. "But seriously, can't you call an Uber or something?"

"No phone and no bank," I reply. "I would let you use mine, but I'm one taco away from overdrafting my account." Her mood begins to change. "Real life sucks, yo."

"Tell me about it." I hand her the foam cup.

"Thanks. I just have one more year of school and if I get this internship at the local brewery I will be set." She pushes her card toward me. "But that is neither here nor there. I have to get going so let's focus on the ride situation."

"Rain, you just told me you barely have enough to pay for a taco. I'll get this." I take the check to settle it up after my shift.

"Thanks, doll. I owe you one." Rain stands. "I'll text Jake. I bet he will let you borrow his ride when he gets in."

"Really?" I ask hopefully.

"Yeah. He's totally cool like that." She punches out a quick text. "Now we wait or, well, you will. I have to get going." She blows me a kiss. "Peace, love and moon babies." She winks before she turns to walk out the door.

"Thanks for everything, Rain," I shout loud enough for her to hear, but not enough to disturb the rest of the lingering lunch crowd.

Turning around, she yells loud enough the whole club can hear. "Jake said yes!" and turns back around and walks out the door.

Score!

Each and every day ends up being better than the last and today feels great!

I'm not sure why I'm nervous. It's only coffee or in my case tea, but still. It's a couple hours of conversation and talking to Lee is easy.

So, why so nervous?

"Who are you?" A girl walks in wearing a little too much makeup and a dress that is a tad too short and way too tight.

"Hi!" I hold out my hand. "I'm Ellie. We haven't met yet."

Ignoring my hand, she puts her personal items in her locker then walks over to the mirror to check her lipstick. "You work dayshift?" She looks at me through the reflection.

"Yeah, I'm just waiting around for Jake."

"Jake?" She spins around.

"What's up?" Jake rounds the corner with helmet in hand.

"Ellie here was just explaining that she was waiting for *you*." She shoots him a look.

"Dammit." He sets his helmet down and slides his sling pack off over his head, pulling his dress shirt tight, every lean inch of muscle on full display. I knew Jake was hot, but I wasn't sure how fit he was until now. "Ellie, I forgot to bring the car. It was a nice day when I stepped out, so I decided to ride."

"Oh." I'm sure my disappointment shows. "It's okay, I can walk."

"Chloe? Can Ellie take your car for a couple hours? She has to be back tonight to perform so she won't be gone long." Jake sets his helmet down and heads to the restroom tucked away in the corner.

"No," she blurts.

My eyes widen in surprise and Jake peeks his head out. "No?" he asks.

"I just had it detailed. Sorry, Ellie." Chloe turns and walks out, leaving Jake and I standing here wondering what the hell just happened.

"I'm sorry, Ellie. Can you wait until tomorrow and I'll just let you borrow my car for a couple days till you figure out your situation?" he says as he runs his hands through his hair, securing every wild hair back in place.

"Thanks Jake, but I don't want to put you out." I lean against the lockers. "Rain will be able to help out tomorrow."

"It's really not a problem." He straightens his tie.

"Let's just see what tomorrow brings." I force a smile. Not because I'm not thankful, because I am. His generosity is genuine and refreshing, but now I have to figure out how I'm going to get to Java Talk so Lee isn't left sitting there, stood up.

"If you change your mind, you know where to find me." He flashes his sexy smirk. "My number, it's posted over there." He points to the bulletin board. "And feel free to use any of the phones."

"Sounds good. Thank you." I push off the lockers and head toward the door. "I better get going. See you tonight."

There are a couple of things I can do right now. I could use one of the phones and call Java Talk and pass along the message once he gets there or I can head out on foot and hope when it's time to leave, he will bring me back.

My feet don't give me time to make the rational decision. I find myself pushing open the back door and pounding the pavement. Mentally, I calculate how long it will take me to get there. Normally, I would punch this info into my GPS, but since I'm at a technical disadvantage, I have no choice but to math.

Fifteen minutes via car. That's with stoplights and traffic. So, by hoofing it on foot, that's what? Maybe double the time? Maybe less if I speed-walk? I got this.

Cary Hart

Lee, don't leave…again.

Chapter Nine

Lee

After two cups of coffee, a brownie and a glass of water, I finally accepted Ellie wasn't coming. *She stood me up.*

Do I blame her? No. I was the one who ran out on her without explanation. Am I surprised? Yes. Ellie seemed like she was excited about this. So, if that is the case, then why am I spending my Friday evening pushing a shopping cart around the grocery store?

I'm twenty-four and this is my life, working and taking care of the one person who devoted their time to taking care of me. It's the circle of life and now I'm doing my part. I have to. I promised my grandfather I would always watch over Grans.

But for how long?

I'm mentally and physically drained and I'm not sure how much longer I can keep this up. If I were to be honest with myself, there are days where I want to run away from here. Leave all my burdens and start over.

Is that who I am?

That's what *she* would do. Am I just like her? Always looking for the next big thing? Starting over when things don't work out according to plan?

She left.
She left.
She left.
You don't leave.
I'm not her.

I'm not. I would never leave my family when they needed me the most. Grans didn't ask for this, just like she didn't ask to raise another child, but she did, and she did it because she loves me. Sometimes, your plans are put on hold for the ones you care about and right now, mine are on pause.

My life, in this moment, is for her. My time, unpredictable. My promises, all used up. That's why I don't do relationships. One-nights are all I can handle.

Why her?

That's the question I have been asking myself since I saw her this afternoon. Why her? Is it because Kyle made me think I could possibly have a new beginning?

I left there on a high, thinking the possibilities were endless. With a promotion in the works and a date with Ellie, I felt like I could take on the world. Today was a good day. Until it came tumbling down.

Katie called me as soon as I left Spotlight. Grans was outside wandering around, confused. She wouldn't let anyone help her and the more neighbors that got involved, the worse it became.

I had a plan in place, people to take care of her. The house is safety-proofed. I'd taken out the stove while I worked on the damage, leaving her with only cold cuts or microwavable food. I took precautions, removing everything from the house that could hurt her.

A flawless plan—or so I thought. It wasn't designed to save Grans from herself.

I was almost there. Then Katie called me back. She was able to coerce Grans inside and calm her down. She reassured me that she had everything under control, but it's Grans. I had to check on her. Then she said the words I never thought I would hear. "Lee, with you here, I'm afraid it will make it worse."

Worse?

How in the world can I make it worse? I make things better. I'm the one who takes care of her. I'm the one who calms her down. I'm the one who made those promises and if I can't even keep them, then who am I?

A failure.

Why did I ask Ellie to coffee? I don't have time for this. She is in a profession where leaving is a guarantee and me…well, my life prevents me from chasing.

But I went anyway.

She didn't show.

So, I left.

And now I'm here.

I'm stocking up on a few items that Grans can fix herself, helping her in the only way I know how at this moment. She isn't a burden.

She's my family.

"Presley, I can't live like this," Grans complains on the other end.

"When are you going to have my kitchen put back together? I need more than microwavable soup and sandwiches."

"Grans—"

"No, Presley. It's like I'm living the college life without all the drunken nights and unprotected sex."

"Grans!" I shout, causing everyone in the aisle to turn my way. "Sorry," I mouth.

"Well, it's true. The only thing I'm missing is that noodle stuff, but wait, you have to boil water for that and you know what it takes to boil water, Presley?" Grans asks, waiting for my answer, laying it on thick to make her point.

"A stove?" I smile at our banter. Just a couple hours ago, Katie wasn't sure Grans would know who I was, and now she's giving me what for. But what she doesn't realize is I'm taking my sweet time on purpose, because I'm not sure how to explain to the woman who used to cook all my meals that I'm afraid for her to do something as easy as boil water.

"That's right. A stove," Grans confirms, and continues needling me.

Taking it all in, I go up and down each aisle, filling my cart with Grans' safe foods. Then I catch someone out of the corner of my eye.

Is that?

"Grans, I have to go," I say in a hushed voice as I park my cart. Stalker mode: on.

Ellie.

I nonchalantly work my way over to the magazine stand and by nonchalantly, I mean I take off full speed so she won't see me. I slide into my destination and reach for the first magazine that I see.

"Nice."

"What?" I glance over to the young pimple-faced kid standing next to me. He's flipping through the *Sports Illustrated* Swimsuit edition.

That out already? Shaking off my thoughts, I try to zone in on my target.

"Page thirty-two has a nice spread. I mean, for a women's fitness magazine."

"Huh?" I flip the magazine I'm holding around to see what he's talking about. *Damn.* The current issue of *Shape*.

"But its hotness factor doesn't even touch this. In this, if you look really close, you can see through her swimsuit." The kid flips through the pages trying to find the one he wants to show me. "See. You can see her—"

"Kenny? I told you to get a gallon of milk." A woman comes speeding down the aisle with a cart full of groceries.

"Oh boy!" The kid, who I'm willing to bet is Kenny, turns to me. "Ready for a show?"

"Oh my God. Put that porn down!" She yanks the magazine from poor Kenny's hands. "Do you know what will happen to you if you look at those things?" she scolds before putting it back on the shelf. I let out a small snicker, which grabs her attention. "You will grow up to be JUST. LIKE. HIM." Kenny's mom jabs her finger in my direction and continues, "You should be ashamed of yourself." She yanks poor Kenny by the arm and I'm left wondering what I was doing in the first place.

Ellie!

Thanks to Kenny, I decide that hiding out only gets you into trouble. So, I put the magazine back where I got it and start to slide my phone into my front pocket when I see Grans' face pop up.

I slide the phone alive to see what she wants. "Yes, Grans?"

"Katie just informed me I'm almost out of those pads. Can you pick me up some? But don't get those diaper ones. I'm not that old and my bladder isn't that bad. I just need those thin things that stick in your drawers. Katie knows what I'm talking about." I hear her pull the phone away and yell, "Katie! Can you tell Presley what kind of pads those are?"

"Grans." I try to grab her attention. I'm back at my cart now and if I'm going to pull this off, I need to get off the phone with her. "Grans, I'll get your pads."

A woman snickers besides me.

Great. Just great.

I cup my hand around the phone and raise my voice a little louder. "Grans, I don't need to talk to Katie."

"Well, then you better get the right ones. Those others—"

"I gotta go." I cut her off, pressing end and heading toward the front of the store where I know I'll find Ellie.

Four lanes down, I see her bending over, plucking cans from the shelf, examining the labels before she puts them in her cart.

"Excuse me." The same woman who snickered just a few seconds ago tries to get by. Moving my cart over to the side, I wait for her to pass before I make my move.

Sliding up behind Ellie, I lower my voice. "Baby have you been eating your Campbell's Soup?" I pause, letting it sink in. "Because you are…" I bite my bottom lip, trying not to laugh at the cheesiness of this one. "…mmm-mmm good."

"Lee!" She jumps up, knocking me right in the chin since I was leaned over her trying to be all sexy and stealth.

"Shit!"

"Oh my God!" She reaches up, hands on either side of my face. The feel of her skin on mine, so soft and smooth, is a touch I could get used to. "Are you okay?" Ellie turns my face side to side. "I can't believe you are here. I started to walk, but gave up—"

"Walk?" I cut her off. "I'm not sure I understand. Why would you walk?"

Dropping her hands, she looks away and mumbles, "I forgot I don't have a car."

I can't help but laugh a little. "Oh, is it in the shop?"

"Not exactly." She turns and begins pushing her cart. "It's a long story."

I reach for mine and pull up beside her, thankful the aisles are wide enough for us to walk side by side. "I have time."

Stopping in the middle of the soup aisle, she looks up at me and confesses. "I dropped out of school to follow my passion. My parents basically disowned me and left me with nothing but a bag of clothes."

"Okay." I nod. "That's kind of a big deal."

"Luckily my friend knew a manager at Spotlight and they hooked me up with not only a job and regular performing schedule, but also a place to live."

"Why didn't you say something? I would have picked you up after work." We continue our stroll down the next aisle. Neither of us is shopping anymore, just enjoying the conversation.

"Remember the part of me forgetting? Well, I literally forgot. I haven't had a need to leave Spotlight since I moved in. They have everything there." She pauses and slows down the cart. "Except for this." She reaches behind me to grab a couple boxes of brownies. "I love the corner pieces."

"Good, we won't have to fight over the pan then. I love the center ones." I turn to grab a couple boxes for myself, hoping that I will eventually have the chance to lure her over to my place. Even though I stay at Grans', I have an apartment above the garage.

"Lee?" She stops the cart, but this time she doesn't turn.

"Yeah?"

"I'm really glad I ran into you."

"Me too."

"Good." She continues on, grabbing a few items off the shelves here and there. "Well, looks like I'm done."

"Me too. Let's go get you checked out."

"Sounds like a plan."

Ellie breaks away first and heads to the front of the store, finding a check-out without a line, and begins to unload her groceries.

"Are you guys together?" The cashier questions when I start to place my items on the belt.

"No." Ellie beats me to it.

"Yes." I put down the divider, making sure our items don't get mixed together. "I mean that's her order and this is mine but put it all on one."

"Lee! You are not paying for my groceries," she protests, digging through her purse, pulling out a wad of cash. "I have tips."

"Yes, you do, but I'm still getting it," I argue.

"Miss, if a man offers to do anything nice, just say 'Thank you' and take it." The cashier nods toward me. "Those kind are hard to come by."

Glancing up at me she does as the cashier suggests and thanks me.

"Don't forget my pads!" Grans hollers.

"Wh-wh-what?" I look around.

"Who was that?" Ellie spins around.

"I think they are checking out," I hear Grans whisper loudly.

I look down at my phone then hold it up to Ellie. "I must have pressed speaker instead of end."

"That's hilarious!" The cashier snorts.

"Grans? Have you been on here the whole time?" I ask.

"Presley Aaron Scott, that doesn't matter, but what does matter is if you got your grans some pads," she demands.

Taking the phone off speaker, I bring the phone up to my ear. "Yes, Grans, I did."

"Good boy. Now, listen closely." She pauses. "You listening?"

"Yes, Grans."

"Good. I want you to take that girl home. Then come straight here. Do not pass go, do not collect two hundred dollars. Do you understand me?"

"Love you, Grans." This time I actually make sure I end the call before I slide the phone into my back pocket.

"That was...fun?" Ellie says, asking in a way that tests if I'm amused or irritated.

"Interesting. For sure." I smile as I slide my card through the little machine. "She wanted to make sure I took you home."

"You don't have to," she quickly responds.

"I know I don't have to, but I want to."

"Here you go." The cashier hands me the receipt and smiles. "You aren't just a pretty face, you are a keeper." She looks at Ellie. "Keep him."

"I'll think about it." Ellie looks over at me and pulls the cart out so I can get through.

"Have a good night you two!" the cashier calls after us.

"She thinks you should keep me." I walk beside Ellie as she pushes our combined cart of groceries out.

"Maybe I will." A slow grin appears right before she hops onto the back of the cart and pushes off. "Last one there!"

"Ellie!" I call after her. "My truck's over here."

Braking, she stops and looks between me and the truck she was heading toward. "I thought this one looked like you." She nods toward the older, slightly worn truck.

"Why's that?" I open the back door and motion her over.

"It just looks like it's well taken care of. You know?" She begins to push the cart across the lot toward my truck. "Whoever owns it sure does love it," she says, moving to the front of the cart, handing me one bag at a time. "It's one of those trucks you keep forever. You know."

"Yeah, I know just the ones." I put the last bag in back and help her in. "They have staying power."

"Yeah." Ellie nods. "Staying power. I like that."

Me too.

Chapter Ten

Ellie

"He's a keeper." Those words, spoken just minutes ago, run through my head on repeat. The clerk noticed what I knew the first night I met him. Lee Scott is someone special. *A keeper.*

"This is it." I set my bags down and dig for my keys.

"I didn't even know this was up here." He glances around the area. "Just two units?"

"Yeah. I guess when they remodeled, the owner decided to keep this a secret level. One apartment was for him, and the other for clients or performers who were passing through town," I say as I try to unlock the door. I push the knob in and up. "Dammit. This thing always gives me trouble."

"What's wrong?" he says, standing too close. His proximity is intoxicating.

"I, um…" I'm unsure of what he asked. So, I say the only thing that comes to mind. "I have to pee."

I have to pee? Kill me now.

Mortified, I cover my face. "Did I just say that?" I say into my palms.

"You did." A low chuckle rumbles form deep within his throat.

"Give me the key."

With my hands still hiding my face, I spread my fingers apart and peek through the cracks. "I don't have to pee," I confess. "You smell good. I couldn't think."

Lee leans in closer, his lips so close I can feel the words he breathes through my fingertips. "You smell good too, Ellie." He raises his hand up and gently removes one of mine followed by the other, bringing it up to his lips for a tender kiss. "But if we don't get these groceries inside, your ice cream will melt."

"Right. Ice cream." I find myself smitten, repeating words. My God, I'm acting like a fool.

"Yes. The key?" He holds out his hand, palm up.

"Oh, right!" I toss them in his direction. If he touches me one more time I'm bound to implode.

With a little jostle, the door opens. "If you have a screwdriver I can fix this right up."

Picking the bags back up, I scoot past him sideways, trying to avoid touching the man because right now all my senses are on high alert. "Um, I don't think I have one, but if you want to come in, feel free to check around." I place the bags on the island and turn, right into Lee. "Where did you come from?"

"Thought you could use some help with these." He leans forward to place the rest of the bags on the counter his body pinning mine against the edge.

"You still smell good."

"I need to wear this every time I see you."

"I think I'm just horny."

The deep rumble of his laugh vibrates next to my ear. "I can take care of that, too."

"I said that out loud, didn't I?"

"Yup."

"That's embarrassing." I try to look away, but he slowly brings my face back to his.

"No, it's not." Our eyes meet, before his drop to my lips. "You know what?"

"Huh?"

"Your lips look lonely." He smiles the sexiest smile I have ever seen.

"They do?"

"Yeah." He licks his lips before continuing, "Would you like them to meet mine?"

Yeah, I sure would...hey wait!

"You dork!" I push him off me, pointing my finger at him as I walk by. "You almost had me."

"Much better than the traditional way, don't you think?" He follows behind me, looking in cabinets and closets.

"Uh-huh." I look over my shoulder. "You keep telling yourself that."

"I think I'd rather keep proving myself right." He winks.

"Did this place come fully furnished?" He opens the coat closet, moving a few things around.

"Yeah. Why?"

He pulls down a little red box. "'Cause I was hoping it would be stocked with one of these." He sets it on the table while he pulls out a couple screwdrivers.

"Oh! The door." I've been so consumed with thoughts of Lee that I forgot his whole purpose for coming in.

"Yeah, it just needs to be adjusted." He kneels down in the open doorway, turning screws to secure the hardware. He wiggles the knob, then stands to open and close the door. "I think this should do it."

"Lee, you didn't have to do that."

He sticks the tools in his back pocket and looks down at me, brows furrowed. "I think we better check out the lock."

"Oh, good idea. Do you want to go outside, or me?"

Locking the door, he goes out into the hall, shutting the door behind him.

What's his problem?

With a turn of the knob, the door flies open. "It's fixed," Lee announces as he stalks toward me, walking me backward until we can't move any farther. My back is against the wall. "I *wanted* to fix it."

"Wha-wha?" I try to get out, but his lips crash down on mine. His tongue expertly invades my mouth, leaving nothing to the imagination.

This kiss is full of passion, exciting all my senses.

Hungry.

Greedy.

He took my mouth as if he owned it. The way he holds me against him, his mouth locked to mine, makes a promise. One of never letting go.

I don't want him to.

Panting, he backs away. "Ellie. I've got to go, but this is not me walking away. I'm not leaving. This is me telling you I'll see you tomorrow."

"Okay." I'm at a loss for words. *And his touch.*

"Okay." He nods, backing away slowly, his grin bigger with each step. "Noon?"

"Sure."

"Oh! I almost forgot." He reaches behind him. "I forgot about these two." He hands me the screwdrivers. "And this." He gives me the keys. "But what I wanted..." He pulls his phone out. "I need to get your number."

"I don't have one. The parents took my phone when I got kicked out."

"Damn." He glances around the room. "Okay." He finds my notebook and pen on the coffee table. "Here is my number." He jots it down. "If for some reason something comes up, call me."

"Thank you."

"Anytime." He nods at the paper. "I'm there if you need me." He backs out the door, which is still open from when he barged in.

"Stay!" I blurt out. "I mean, I'm performing tonight. Stay and watch." I try to plead my case in getting him to stay.

"I wish I could, but Grans is waiting on her—"

"Pads?" I interrupt, causing us both to laugh at the memory.

"I was going to say groceries, but yeah, those too." He gives me one more sexy smirk before he finally turns and leaves, but this time, I know it's with a *promise* of tomorrow.

Chapter Eleven

Lee

Something shifted tonight and I'm not sure when or how it happened, but I felt it and I know damn well she felt it too.

That kiss.

It replays in my head over and over again. My mouth on hers. Devouring it. Needing more, but not taking it.

She asked me to stay. That was my chance to find out who she is, but staying meant breaking a promise I already made, and I couldn't risk that. So, I did the only thing I could. I left with another promise—that I'll be back tomorrow.

With work, Grans and the back and forth, I can barely manage as it is. And now that I've found someone I want to spend time with, I find myself thinking about what I should be doing and what I want, but it's not about me. It's never been about me.

Ellie wasn't a part of the plan, but I want her to be. *Damn, I want her to be.* I just have to figure out how in the world I can keep my promise to one, while wanting to make *all* the promises to the other—and keep them.

Things are looking up. With the pending promotion, the home nurse, extra help from the neighbors, and now Ellie, I feel as if I can accomplish anything. That no matter what happens, I can deal with it.

Almost home, I try to push the thoughts of Ellie away and focus on Grans. She's made it a point of telling me how sick and tired she is of the food I've been forcing her to eat and honestly, I don't blame her. I can't keep using the fire damage as an excuse to keep the kitchen out of order. I'm scared of what will happen when I'm gone though. Will she burn herself? Forget what she is cooking? I have no clue, but I do know that me taking my time getting things put back together is a way of controlling the situation, but just like the disease, you can't really control it. I know I need to deal with it, but for now, I think I've come up with a solution.

Pulling in, I see all the lights are on. Last time I came home to this, she was searching through every room in the house for a necklace my grandfather gave her on their tenth wedding anniversary. The memory of that day is vivid.

"Where is it? Where did it go?" Grans is frantic, searching through all the drawers, tossing clothes around the room, talking to herself. "It has to be here somewhere." She turns, finally noticing me.

"What's going on?"

"Oh, honey. I'm so sorry." She rushes over, wrapping her arms around me. "I lost it."

"Lost what?" I'm confused.

"The necklace." She pulls back, running her fingers through my hair, something she always used to do to my grandfather.

"Which one?"

"The heart locket, the one you got me for our tenth wedding anniversary." Tears begin to stain her face.

"That I got you?" I'm still unaware of what is going on or what necklace she is talking about. I've never bought her one, and I never felt like I should; that was something my grandfather would do for each anniversary. It was something special between them.

Between them. No…

"Oh, Paulie, I'm so sorry. I lost it," she apologizes to her late husband, my grandfather, thinking I'm him.

Me.

The doctors tried to explain and I listened the best I could, but I thought I had time to do the research. To talk to the therapists who could help me deal with the situations when they eventually happened. Because they would happen. I didn't listen. I didn't prepare. I should have. Because this moment, no matter how prepared you are, is devastating.

Pushing her away, I turn and try to figure out what to do. I pace the room, searching for the right thing to say, to do.

"Paulie, please don't be mad." She covers her face as sobs rack her body.

I need to find the necklace. Where would it be?

"Honey, I had it on, or I thought I did." She begins to follow me around the room, not giving me the space I need to think.

"Just stop!" I roar, the situation too much for me to bear.

Grans' eyes go wide with fear; she collapses to the floor, curls up in a ball and cries, repeating something that I can't make out, over and over again.

I did this. I caused her to fear my grandfather. Panic sets in. What happens now? Did I change her past by not handling the situation the right way? Will she think my grandfather, who adored her, who never raised his voice once, yelled at her?

I can't take it.

"I love you. Please don't go. Please don't leave me. I didn't mean to." *Her chant is more clear, and louder.*

I have to find it. Walking around the room, stepping over clothes, I begin to search all the places I thought it could have been, but I find nothing.

The closet. When grandfather passed, she packed away all of his things and stored them in the closet. The thought of her having to donate his things was too final for her. So, we spent hours organizing and boxing up his stuff.

Throwing open the doors of her walk-in closet, I search for the small, metal, fireproof box that I bought for her to store all my grandfather's prized possessions. Working my way from the back to the front, I finally find it, next to his worn-out house slippers. I smile at the memory of him sliding them on every morning on his way to the kitchen where Grans would have one egg over easy, a piece of toast—lightly toasted, but heavy on the butter—and a cup of black coffee, while he read the morning paper.

Opening the box, I see all the necklaces my grandfather bought her, one for every anniversary. How could I have forgotten? Grans lost a lot of weight after my grandfather's passing. Worried she would lose her wedding ring, she took hers and his and put them on a worn-out, gold-plated chain he bought her for their first year together. She put all the other ones away and had worn those symbols of their promises every day since.

I questioned why that necklace, but she just said it's the reason for all the other ones, but this one meant more. Too poor to buy something of value, he bought that one for a few dollars and surprised her with it on their first anniversary, with a promise of nice ones to come.

Gently untangling the years of memories, I find the one she was searching for and try to right my wrong.

"Jeanie," I speak the name I heard my grandfather say so many times. *"Look what I found."*

"Paul! You found it." She pushes herself up off the floor, making her way to me. Turning, she lifts up her hair. *"Will you?"*

"Sure, Jeanie." I slide the memories around her neck and clasped it in place.

"Thank you, Paul! I love it as much as the day you bought it for me," Grans says, making her way over to the mirror, admiring the necklace she thought was lost.

I can't stay in here any longer. I need air. "Jeanie, I'm going to work in the garage."

"Okay, honey," she says, waving me off.

Almost out the door she calls after me. "Tell Sammy-Jo it's time for lunch."

I cringe at the name I haven't heard in a couple years. One that I could go a lifetime without hearing again.

A knock on my window startles me. Katie stands there, just watching me.

How long have I been sitting here?

Swinging open the door, I gather the bags.

"I saw you just sitting out here. I thought maybe you could use a hand." She reaches in and grabs a couple bags. "I thought you were just getting a few things?" She laughs at the bags piled in the back seat.

"Well, Grans complained, and this time I listened." I smile.

Heading toward the house, Katie fills me in on the events from earlier. How she found Grans, what she did to calm her down. Luckily, Katie was at home and has the patience of Job.

"Hey, Lee." She reaches for the door. "There's something else that I think you should know before—"

"Here let me get that." I take the door from her, letting her inside first.

"Lee. I think—" She turns suddenly, eyes wide.

"Katie, what's wrong? What aren't you telling me?" I push past and call out for Grans as I throw the sacks on the table. "Grans are you—"

"Shhhh, she just laid down."

A woman who I haven't seen in a couple years comes walking down the hall. A vision that should be familiar, yet is so foreign.

"Mom? What are you doing here?"

"What am I doing here?" She takes a step closer.

I raise my hand, a silent warning not to come any closer.

"Katie, did you call her?" My voice catches as I turn to face the woman who has helped me so much over the past few years. Someone who I have counted on numerous times and without question was always there.

"Lee, I promise, I didn't." She sets the bags down and comes to stand in front of me. "I wouldn't."

"Okay." I nod.

My mom has always been in and out of my life since I was born, chasing a father who I never knew. Then when I was seven she left for good, only coming back when she needed something.

"Get out," I mumble, turning around, facing the last person I want to see tonight. My mom is checking her reflection in the stainless-steel toaster, the only appliance I didn't remove since it basically has a built-in timer.

"So, I was thinking—"

"Get out," I say a little louder.

"That maybe we could do something, just the two of us," she continues as if I hadn't interrupted. "Maybe do a little catching up?"

"Get! Out! Now!" The anger in my voice vibrates through every cell in my body.

"Presley—" she pleads.

"Do not call me that!" I swing the door open. "Actually, don't call me at all. Leave!"

"Lee, I'm not going anywhere." She stands her ground.

"Fine. You leave me no choice." I stomp over to where she is, heart racing, adrenaline pumping. "You made your decision when you left." I reach for her arm, but she jerks away.

"Lee, you don't know what you're talking about." She tries to place her hand on my chest. The touch is meant to calm, but instead it infuriates me.

"What's there to know?" I get in her face and say the words I have wanted to say each and every time she *popped in*. "No one wants you here," I snarl, my voice laced with venom.

"I do." Grans comes strolling down the hall. "I called her. I want her here."

I have never felt so much betrayal as I do right now. Grans, who has worked a lifetime to heal the broken heart this woman shattered, invited the exact same woman back to do it all over again. *Why?*

"Presley, my dear, sweet boy." Grans pushes her way in front of me, separating me from my mom. "I called her last week and asked her to come home. I need help," she says as she looks up, trying to blink away the tears.

Wrapping my arms around the woman who was a mom in every

sense of the word, I reassure her. "Grans, I can take care of you."

"I know you can, but you shouldn't have to." She brings an arm up between us and pats my chest. "I knew what I was getting into with you. I chose to take care of you, but you..." She shakes her head. "You didn't have a choice."

"Grans." I push away. "What are you saying?"

"I'm saying." She takes a step forward, placing her small, fragile hand over my wounded heart. "This. It deserves to beat, to live. Presley, it deserves to love." She exhales, closing her eyes.

"I am. I'm doing all those things." I start to count off on my hands. "I just got a promotion, I have people asking me about my furniture, I met this girl."

"Yes! That—it's what I want for you." Grans takes my hand, holding it between both of hers. "I want you to experience what I had with your grandfather. I want you to learn to live life and love it, not be bogged down with a schedule. You are a twenty-four-year-old man with a curfew, because of me." Grans turns her head, silently speaking to my mom. "I don't want to be your promise anymore."

"Grans." I begin to pace the room. "You aren't just a promise. You are my *mom*. You are everything to me. I can't lose you. Let me have this." I stop in front of her begging. "Let *me* be there for *you*."

"Lee." My mom pushes herself off the counter. "I'm not here to take your place. I'm here to help." To everyone else, I'm sure she seems sincere, putting on a show as she reaches for Grans' hand, but I know better. "I'm here to help you."

"Thank you, Sammy-Jo." Gran gives her a tight smile.

Watching their exchange, I can see that they have a history. A whole lifetime before me, but I still can't help but think she has an ulterior motive for doing this.

"You're welcome, Mother." She pulls Grans in for a side hug, rubbing circles on her back as she continues. "Presley and I will have a little talk and work all this out."

"Sure, *Mom*. Let's get right on that." I head for the door, Katie stepping out of my way. "In private. I have a few things I want to get off my chest." I'm out the door before she has a chance to decline.

I should have stayed. I should have called Katie and asked her to spend the night with Grans because right now, I could have Ellie wrapped up in my arms. Instead I'm here, trying to protect my future from my past.

Chapter Twelve

Lee

I have no clue who she thinks she is, but I'll be damned if she thinks she's going to walk into this house and claim it as her home, because she's sadly mistaken.

"Presley." My mom quickly follows me out. "I think you—"

"I'm going to stop you right there," I snap, standing still, careful not to get too close. "You don't get to call me that."

"It's your name."

I laugh. I laugh because it's her only defense. I laugh because she thinks I want a name she gave me. I laugh because I'm here, in this situation, arguing with a woman who thinks she has the right.

"Yes, you are exactly right. It's the name you gave your child. The same child you abandoned while you were off trying to…what was it you called it? Oh yeah." I bring my hands up, making air quotes. "*Make it big*. Well guess what? The name went when you did."

"Lee," she pleads, as if it really matters. This woman doesn't have a caring bone in her body.

"Hey, you're a fast learner." I applaud.

"Okay. You know what, Lee, why don't you get whatever you have against me off your chest, because I'm not going to get a word in edgewise until you do." She throws up her hands, walks across the front porch, and takes a seat on the second step. "Have at it, son."

Son.

I roll my head from side to side, trying to shake it off. *Son.* It's not a term of endearment, it's not even a name. When she says it I feel like she's marking me. She has no right to me. Everything I have is because of *her* parents.

I open then close my mouth, trying to find the right words. If I'm going to do this, fight with her, then I'm going to get some answers in the process.

"I hate you," I seethe. "I hate you for loving the industry more than you love your family. I hate you for being so fucking obsessed with making it that you flung yourself at every goddamned tour bus. I hate that you don't even know who my father is. Fucking your way through a band. Hoping to trap just one. How did that work for you, *Mom?*"

I clasp my hands behind my head. I just watch. Daring her to say something.

"At first, Grans lied to me. When you were gone weeks at a time, she told me you were on tour with these big bands. That you were, you are going to love this." I laugh hysterically, taking a few steps closer, then stopping. "Grans said," I bend over, resting my hands on my knees to look her straight in the eye, "you are so talented and that someday you are going to be somebody *I* can be proud of."

Pushing myself upright, I pace back and forth, catching glimpses of her each time I pass by until I stop right in front of her. We lock eyes. "ALL. LIES."

Inhaling, I wait.

Nothing.

Exhaling, I wait.

Nothing.

"Maybe I'm being too hard on you?" I tap my finger rapidly against my lips before I continue. "Maybe I should be thanking you?" I close the distance between us. "Mind if I have a seat?" I point to the empty spot next to her.

Not saying a word, she searches my face for a hint of what I'm doing, then scoots over.

"Thanks, *Mom*." I reach over and squeeze her knee. "Thank you." I pause. "Thank you for leaving and giving me the opportunity to have the best parents anyone could have asked for. For allowing me to grow up feeling loved. Every. Single. Day. For having someone teach me how to work hard. How to believe in myself. To treat others how you want to be treated. To be there when someone needs you." I give her knee once last squeeze before I reach up and with one finger, turn her face to mine and say the two words I know will burn. *"To stay."*

I stand and quickly turn around, walking backward. "So, thank you." I throw my head back to the night sky, hands clenched in the air, and shout, "Best. Mom. Ever."

"You spoiled little brat." She's up and running toward me and shoves me when she reaches me. "You think you know?" She pushes me again. "You have no idea about me or my life."

"That's right, Mom. How would I?" I grab her hands as she goes to shove me again. "You left. I had no choice but to *not* know you."

"God!" She squints her eyes, letting out a deep breath. "I was so young and made so many mistakes. I know I messed up with you, but I wasn't right. In here." She taps her temple. "Or here." She grabs her chest.

"I needed you." It's a simple response. Not one of rage as moments ago, but a simple statement from a boy who desperately wanted his mom.

"I know." She shrugs a shoulder, her lips tight, and tears escape. "And I regret every single day I was gone because it turned out what I thought I was missing wasn't what I was running toward. It's what I was running from. It was you."

"Why now, Mom? Why come back?"

"Your Grans called. Made me an offer I couldn't refuse."

"There it is. I knew it." I throw my hands up. "You know what? You really did have me there for a minute." I walk past her. "Maybe you should have tried your hand at acting because I'm pretty sure that was an Oscar-worthy performance." I'm almost to the steps before I turn around and unload on her again. "It wasn't enough you had to take all Grandfather's insurance money, but you couldn't even come back to help Grans? You had to have an offer? What? Is she paying you? Write you back into the will? Ohhhhh, the house? What is it, Mom? What's the offer?" I ask the million-dollar question and reach out for the railing to brace myself for the answer.

"Oh Presley." She edges her way toward me.

"Lee," I bark out.

"Lee, you have no clue what you're talking about."

"Enlighten me."

"The insurance money? I guess you can say I used it. Your Grans," she points toward the house, "used it to pay for my rehab. The offer? Was you."

"Me? I don't get it." I look toward the house, needing a break from her lies.

"I didn't leave you because I wanted to. I left because I had no choice. They gave me an ultimatum. Lose the drugs or lose you," she confesses, now standing right in front of me. "I was sick. I was sick, broke and had no place to go. I tried rehab. I exhausted all their resources, drained their savings. At the time I thought they didn't love me and taking you was their punishment, but now I know it was the only thing they could do. Lee, honey, I had to *want* to help myself before I *could* be helped."

"Then why didn't you come back after rehab?" I look down at the woman I thought I knew, but in reality, I don't know her at all. I'm beginning to think I don't know the woman inside the house either.

"I was afraid," she confesses. She wraps her arms around my waist and my body stiffens. "Of rejection."

"Mom," I whisper.

"I know I made mistakes. I missed out on all those years with not only you, but my parents, too." Tears begin to soak my shirt, but I don't care. I let her continue. "My father died thinking I was the same person you thought I was. And my mother, whom I have begged time and time again to forget the past, is not only going to forget it, but she is going to lose the only good I had with them as well." Her confession is too much for her to bear and her body begins to tremble as sobs rack her body.

Tonight, everything has changed, yet it's still the same. At a loss for words, I find myself doing the only thing I can do, I hug her back. I comfort the woman who was never there to comfort me, because of the woman in that house. The same woman who taught me compassion but also robbed me of a life of truth.

Chapter Thirteen
Ellie

A soft rap on the door has me jumping out of bed and checking the time.

He said noon!

Running into the bathroom, I dig around for a hair tie and pull my hair up on top of my head as the rapping continues to get louder and louder.

"Coming!" I holler as I search through last night's clothes to find a bra.

There it is.

I slide it on as the knock becomes a pounding. Hurrying, I down a cap full of mouth wash, not even bothering to spit it out. I run to the door, sliding to a stop.

I take a second to calm my breathing, place a hand on the frame and slowly open the door. "I thought you said—"

"About time!" Rain pushes past me, bag in one hand and a drink in the other. "I've been basically walking the streets all morning picking up goodies for you."

"Is that for me?" I point to the cup in her hand.

"Uh-huh!" She smiles. "I'll give you one guess as to what it is." Rain waves it in front of me as she plops down on the bed.

I climb on and sit cross-legged in front of her, ready for whatever she has for me. "Ginger tea with two teaspoons of honey?"

"Oh shit! Are you playing this weekend?" She doesn't wait for my answer. "I made sure to check with Jake this morning. Called him up and demanded to know your schedule. He said you were off, but maybe he was telling me to fuck off." She sticks her hand out for me to take the cup.

"I'm off the whole weekend, but I'm pretty sure the f-bomb was dropped before the off." I let out a little chuckle, grabbing the cup.

"It's your favorite," she replies while digging through her bag full of presents.

"Caramel Macchiato with coconut milk, extra caramel, extra whip?" I question, even though I already know the answer. I love those things, but my old voice coach used to swear drinking milk creates phlegm—a huge no-no on performance day. All the research I had done said otherwise, but I wasn't about to chance it.

"Yup!" She bounces up and down, apparently finding what she was looking for. "And LEMON POUND CAKE."

"Sweet!" I reach out, but Rain yanks her hand back. "They only had one, but since I'm an amazing friend," she tosses it at me, "I'm going to let you have it."

Leaning toward her, I inhale and bust out in laughter. "You had a sausage, cheddar, egg sandwich, didn't you?"

She puts her hands up and shrugs. "I couldn't help it. Last night they made me eat this leafy stuff with vegetables."

"You mean a salad?" I tear off a piece of lemon loaf and pop it in my mouth, then let a moan escape.

"That too, but I'm telling you, last night was some weird shit. Even for my parents." She sets the bag down in front of me. "They had me wrapped in a white sheet, toga-style. Which, I do have to say, I looked really good. So, if you know of any toga or Halloween parties, I'm game. Anywho, that is neither here nor there." She hops off the bed and lies on the floor. "They had me lying in the middle of the garden. Like this." Rain then sits up, rolls over and sits on her knees and continues, "And then they did this whole worshipping thing, where they bowed down, but when they came up, they squealed like pigs and their hands were flailing everywhere." She continues to mock them, causing me to spit my coffee everywhere.

"Rain!" I laugh.

"Welcome to my life." She climbs back on the bed. "Aren't you going to open the rest?" She nods toward the bag.

"I was waiting for the show to finish." I give her a big, toothy grin while I dig my hand into the bag and pull out the first item. "Kitchen Lemon Soap! My favorite!" I bounce up and down, causing the bag to fall over and the rest of the contents to fall out.

I can't help it. I love all things lemons. Candy, cookies, cake, soap. Hell, I even love lemon-scented cleaner.

"You idiot!" She tosses the empty bag over her shoulder.

"Hey! You better pick that up. I'm my own housekeeper now," I tease while I go through the rest of the gifts. "Vanilla ChapStick." I pop off the lid and glide the balm over my lips, smacking them together.

"I figured you may need some more since I never see you without it."

"I'm on my last stick. Thanks." I lean over, placing it on my nightstand. "Let's see. A package of my favorite picks and a box of condoms." My eyes widen in surprise. "Rain! What are these for?"

"Oh, baby girl, if I have to explain that to you, then we have some bigger problems." She cranes her neck, trying to look into the kitchen. "Do you have any bananas?"

"Rain!" I smack her arm. "I know what they are for."

"Whew! That could have been uncomfortable." She takes a deep breath and exhales. "Okay." She slaps the bed. "I have something else for you." She pats down the down comforter. "It has to be here somewhere." Rain lifts up her leg. "Here it is." She pulls out a small, black bag. "And here you go."

Looking between the bag and her, I ask, "What's this?" I take the bag and open it to find a new cell phone. "Rain!"

"I hate that I can't text you in the middle of the night."

"You just hate you can't track me on that app you installed on my old phone." I laugh, ripping open the box.

"Hey, it was for your protection."

"Sure." I realize that just yesterday she had barely enough money for a taco. How in the hell could she afford all this? "Rain?"

"Mmm-hmm?" She hops off the bed, picking up the bag and the rest of the trash.

"Where did you get the money to pay for all this stuff?" I hold up my phone. "This phone probably cost—"

"It's one of those disposables, but they assured me that when and if you decide to go with a provider, your number will switch over."

"You asked questions. How grown-up of you." I nod. "But seriously. Where?"

"Geesh. Why can't you just take the gifts and shut up." She reaches for the condom box. "Maybe I'll just keep these."

"Not a chance." I grab them and throw them in my nightstand.

"Ohhhh, so Mr. Rough Hands really is Mr. Doable?" Rain smirks.

"Changing the subject. Nice." I put my hands on my hips. "The money?"

"Fine." She huffs. "Last night my parents got into their special herbs. You know, the ones that have their own 'special' house?"

"Ohhhhh!" I nod, curious as to where she is going with this. Her parents have been known to light up a time or two—a day.

"Well, this stuff must have been good because I was joking around and told them I needed three hundred dollars to donate to an El Nino Go Fund Me page and they gave it to me." She starts laughing hysterically. "You get it? You're El and your bank account is Nino."

"You dork. Nino is boy in Spanish. I think you meant nada." I fall back into the pillows and let out a sigh.

"Same difference." She comes to lay by me.

I turn my head to take a look at the girl who has become like a sister to me, a no-questions-asked friend. As crazy as she is, I can't imagine her not being in my life. "Thank you for everything."

"It's just a phone, and I did it for purely selfish reasons." She reaches over, grabbing it from my hand.

"Hey!"

"I'm programming my number in," she defends herself, before puffing up her hair, making a face, and snapping a cute selfie for her contact image.

"Seriously if it weren't for you, I don't know where I would be right now." I can't help but recall the day I lost everything.

"I can tell you. You would be homeless or hijacking your way to Nashville." She climbs out of bed and starts to grab her things.

"You mean hitchhiking?" I call after her.

"Yeah! That too." She slings her bag over her shoulder. "Listen, I have to get going. Do you want to meet up later?

"Actually, Lee is coming to pick me up at noon." I roll over, pulling the comforter with me.

"That's an hour from now." She holds up her phone. "You better get a move on it. You still smell like last night." Rain pinches her nose, while continuing. "Love ya! Text me."

"Back at ya!" I call after her.

As much as I want to lie here, the need to see Lee is greater. Rolling out of bed, I head to the bathroom where I already have everything laid out. Glancing in the mirror, I notice I look different.

Content.

Chapter Fourteen

Lee

I couldn't sleep. I tried, but given the turn of events last night, I didn't see it happening anytime soon. So, I did the one thing I knew would calm my nerves. I went to the garage to fiddle around, see where the night took me. I just didn't expect it to take me through the night and into the early morning.

I'm exhausted, hungry, and my body is begging for sleep, but then I think of *her* and it awakens. Just thinking about that kiss keeps me feeling alive.

"I thought I would find you out here." Grans walks in with a thermos full off coffee and pours me a cup.

"I couldn't sleep." I continue to sand, avoiding eye contact. After last night I'm a little angry, but I get it, I do. She was trying to help her only child, while at the same time protecting me from a mother who was obviously unstable. How can I be mad at that?

"So I heard." She rubs her face, then pours herself a cup. "I think I owe you an apology."

"Grans, don't," I plead, looking her in the eyes. I cannot go through this again.

"Presley, I love you with all my heart, but seeing you like this is killing me." She walks over and forces the cup into my hand. "Drink."

"Thanks." I bring the mug up to my lips, listening as she continues.

"I didn't tell you because I wasn't sure if she would even come back."

"Grans." I set the cup down and begin to busy myself. "She stayed gone because of you."

Did she?

"Yes." She nods. "And no." She places a hand on my shoulder. "Presley, dear."

Presley. She's the only person I allow to call me by my given name. When she says it, it doesn't hurt.

"Your mother told me what she said last night and it's true, but we cared about you as if you were our own son. The moment she walked out is the moment she didn't come first. You did." Grans begins to cry. "I don't know how long I have. My mind, as much as we'd both like to think otherwise, it's going."

Pulling her into my arms, holding her tight, I comfort Grans the way she always has comforted me, loved me.

Unconditionally.

"I know." I try to hold back the tears but fail miserably. This disease not only takes your memories, it destroys who you are. You lose all sense of reason. So, while she is with me, I'm going to hug her tighter, love her harder and make sure she gets the best care possible. Whether it's with me or with the best memory care center, either way I will protect her with everything I am.

"I love you."

"I love you too, my sweet boy," Gran says as she pulls away. She reaches up, placing a hand on each side of my face. "That is why I called her. I know I need help."

"Grans, I can—" I try to interrupt, but instead she shushes me.

"I know you can. You have showed that time and time again, but right now, I need you to take care of you." She pokes me in the chest, and I shake her hand off. "My, my—construction has been good for you." She winks.

Hands on hips, I puff out my chest and deepen my voice. "I like to think so."

"Oh geez." Grans rolls her eyes. "What I was *trying* to say is you need to get out more, find a girl, get married and have a family of your own."

I pull her back to me. "There is plenty of time for that. Right now, I just want to spend time with—"

"There isn't," Grans cuts in. "I'm running out of time and I want to *see* you happy. I know I won't get to experience those things with you, but if I could just see you do some of them—live your life for *you*—that would make this shitty situation more tolerable." Grans smiles. Reaching up again, she squeezes my cheeks together. "So, tell me about this girl you met."

For the next half hour or so we talk all about Ellie. How we met, why I left, the grocery store and the kiss. Grans sits patiently, taking it all in, asking questions here and there. Being here, like this, is what I'll miss the most.

Needed.

Ellie

I have played in front of hundreds of people. Traveled across the country without knowing a single soul. But this? Waiting for Lee to pick me up has my nerves shot to hell.

It's not like I've never been on a date before, I have. Lots of them. Well, not exactly lots. I'm not that type of girl, but if a guy asked me out, I would go.

Lee's different. I'm not sure why, but I find myself hanging on his every word, mentally begging him not to leave. Hell, last night I was one step away from throwing myself at him.

So, now I'm here, standing outside of Spotlight, wondering if I made the right decision. Maybe I should have waited upstairs or by the bar. "Ugh!" I throw my head back. I hate that I'm second-guessing myself.

"Hey, you," Lee calls out as he comes walking around the corner.

"I was excited!" I blurt.

Damn it! I need to get my mouth under control. If I would have waited upstairs this wouldn't have been a problem.

Lee chuckles as he walks up to me, hands in pockets. "Was? Should I be worried?"

"Oh God!" I bury my head in my hands. "I—damn it. I can't even form a sentence when I'm around you."

Lee's hands are on mine, slowly peeling them away from my face.

"Now, what were you saying?" he asks with a toothy grin.

He knows what he does to me so why is he making me say the words? I narrow my eyes. "Fine. I *am* excited. So much that I didn't want to wait for you to come up."

"So, I make you nervous?" He reaches for my hand.

"Yeah."

Before I can say anything else, he pulls me into him, his lips softly caressing mine.

Top—*lick*.

Bottom—*suck*.

Top—*pull*.

Bottom—*nip*.

Repeating, falling into a rhythm my lips can sing to.

Nerves—vanish.

Butterflies—flutter.

This man has a way with me.

Breaking away, our eyes open. Lee's mouth slowly turns into a smirky smile. Mine follows.

"Better?" He reaches out and tucks a few wild hairs behind my ear.

I slowly nod, my eyes never leaving his.

"Great. My truck is just over there." He points across the road. "You ready?"

I open my mouth to speak. Luckily, I'm able to form a sentence. "Yup."

Close enough.

"Ellie?" He takes my hand in his.

"Yeah?" I reply. I'm rocking this communication thing.

"I'm excited too," he admits as he brings our hands up to his mouth, kissing the top of mine. "And every single time I see you, you manage to take my breath away."

Opening my mouth and then closing it again, I decide words are no longer needed. I let him guide me across the street.

Everything Lee Scott does has meaning and I look forward to exploring his definitions.

Chapter Fifteen

Ellie

"I love your place." I walk around the front room while he maneuvers his way through the kitchen.

"Thanks. My grandfather and I started to fix it up when I was in high school." He reaches up to grab some kind of spice from the top shelf, causing his fitted tee to rise just enough for me to get a sneak peek of those two little dimples that sit right above his perfect ass.

"So the plan was for you to always live here?" I head into the kitchen and find a place out of his way.

"Not at all. This was supposed to be a rec room, a place for me to hang with all my friends. But then he got sick and I got a job." He reaches into the fridge, pulling out a package of mozzarella.

"I'm sorry." I take a few steps closer. "Have you always worked construction?" I fiddle with the fresh basil on the counter.

"Yeah." He begins to mince a couple cloves of garlic, or maybe he is dicing. I'm not really sure since my cooking skills are those of a college student. "Because of age restrictions, I had to start with the cleanup crew, but as I worked my way up."

"Where do you see—" I try to ask another question, but Lee quickly cuts me off.

"Three question limit," he states.

"Oh, I'm sorry," I quickly respond.

Laying down the knife, he walks over to the sink and washes his hands. All the while I want to crawl into a little hole and die.

Coming to stand across from me, he leans back against the island, reaches out and pulls me to him. His hands on my hips, he says, "My turn to ask three questions."

"Oh? Is this a game?"

"You mean like strip poker?" He nods over to the pan of sauce he just started. "We probably should keep all clothes on until after dinner."

"You're a mess." I grab hold of his wrists, sliding my hands down to his as I remove them from my hips. "I meant do you do this all the time?" I take a step back to separate myself from the disappointment of his answer, but as quickly as I take a step, he takes one forward.

"Ellie, I have never wanted to know someone more than I want to know you. The questions? I just need to know. I'm a greedy bastard who wants to know all your secrets." He pulls me in, kissing me on the top of my head before he lets me go. "This wasn't a game, but now that I think of it, it's ours. Mine and yours."

"So, we have a thing?"

"We do." He winks. "You ready to be grilled?" He picks up the knife, waiting for my answer.

I nod toward the knife. "Should I be scared? Because I just watched *Silence of the Lambs* last week and I feel the need to ask if you are literally or figuratively asking."

Shaking with laughter, he replies, "Figuratively."

"Thank God." I hold my hand to my chest.

"I want to know everything, so I'm going to ask you something that has actually been bothering me."

"Now I'm really worried."

"Who is Eloise Hawthorne?" He reaches for the herbs and begins chopping, looking up at me through his lashes, waiting for my answer.

"Going big, huh?" I gulp. "It's my given name, but when I started to perform, I took the stage name Ellie Thorne.

"Then why not introduce yourself as Eloise?" Lee asks the question I would've told him that night, but he ran off.

"It's common for performers to take stage names. Sometimes they even take it as far as legally changing them, but for me, I just wanted to forget Eloise Hawthorne."

"Why?" It's a simple question with such a complex answer.

"I'm going to try and give you the CliffsNotes version."

"No, I want the full scoop." He waves at the mess. "This may take a while. We have time."

"Speaking of which, why so much food?"

"Ask me that question when it's your turn." He twists around and wipes the contents of the cutting board into the pot.

"Okay." I give him a funny look.

"Do you mind stirring while I put the casserole together? Plus, I just want you closer." He grins at me.

"You have a dangerous smile." I flash him one of mine as I step in behind him.

"How so?"

"Time will tell, Scott. Time will tell," I kid as I tilt my head back, but Lee surprises me with a quick peck to the nose.

"Now spill it," he demands.

Taking a deep breath, I spend what seems like forever filling Lee in on everything from my parents' situation to boarding school to being forced to go to college, leaving all my hard work and dreams behind.

"So that is me, in a nutshell. I finally woke up and realized my life was exactly that, *my* life, but when I did something about it they disowned me. Left me with nothing but a bag full of clothes." I point to myself. "Ellie Thorne, D.O.B.: now!"

"Hi!" He spins around, pulling me into his arms once again—a move I'm beginning to like.

"Hi!" I respond, waiting for him to crash his lips down on mine, but it doesn't come. Instead he releases me and goes back to putting the casserole together.

"Want to see my garage?" he says over his shoulder.

"Garage?"

"Yeah. Just let me get this pan in the oven." He reaches around me, turning the sauce down.

"Okay."

"You are going to love this." He snatches up my hand and pulls me along.

"If I ask what it is, will it count toward my questions?"

"Yup."

"You know what? I think I love surprises."

"Good answer!"

Lee is standing in front of the door, taking deep breaths. "Okay, I didn't think I would be this nervous, but if I'm being honest, I'm freakin' out a little here."

"I'm sure whatever is behind this door, it's amazing," I try to reassure him.

Lee reaches behind him, opens the door and takes a step to the left so I can go in. "Go easy on me."

"Aren't you coming in?" I stand still, teetering between going in and staying out.

"Yeah. I'm just giving you a head start." He looks at me sideways.

"Don't believe you." I snake my arm around his, pulling Lee into the garage with me. "See, is that so bad?" I let go of his arm and face his work space. "Lee!" I gasp.

"That bad, huh?" He's in front of me, making sure he sees every single reaction.

"No." I walk over to a rocking chair first. "These are amazing." I look back at him. "Did you do all these?"

He nods.

"And this too." I head over to a bedroom set, running my hand over the bed post. "The detail is incredible."

"Thanks. Sometimes I take special orders and make them in my spare time," he confesses, walking to a piece that has a sheet thrown over it.

"Have you thought about opening your own store?"

"Yeah, but right now, I need something that is consistent."

"I get that," I say as I go over to stand next to him. "What's this one?"

"Hmm, I'm not sure." His dangerous, sexy, smirk of a smile is back. "Let's check it out." He gently pulls the sheet off.

"Lee! Is this..." I reach out to touch it, but I'm afraid I will mess it up. "Can I?"

"Sure. I still need to stain and seal it, but go right ahead."

"Lee, when did you make this?" I look between him and the wooden guitar stand, still amazed that he made this, for *me*.

"Last night," he replies, his voice barely audible.

"Last night?" I ask to make sure I heard him right.

"Yeah."

"When did you sleep? This...it has so much detail. The curves, the lines; it had to have taken forever."

"I didn't sleep."

"Not at all?"

"Nope. I couldn't."

The sentiment overwhelms me. This man, who I just met, stayed up all night making something so perfect. Equal parts me and him combined in a piece of furniture that he made with his hands.

"Thank you, Lee. Thank you! Thank you! Thank you!" I jump into his arms, feathering tiny kisses all over his face, causing Lee to shake with laughter again.

But those kisses begin to slow and my need for more becomes urgent. Legs wrapping around his waist, I'm closer than I have ever been. My fingers inch their way up his neck, tugging at his hair as his mouth opens for me.

Last night he may have claimed my mouth, but today, it's my turn. I lick, suck and twirl my tongue around his. Devouring every moan, inhaling every breath. He is mine.

"This—we should…" He tries to break away, but I kiss his neck, then bite down. "Fuck it." He walks us over to his desk and turns around so that he's sitting and I'm straddling him. Pulling at his hair while his hands snake up my shirt, I begin to move. My body needs the friction, needs him.

"So you liked it?" He breathes the words as he kisses up my neck.

"So much," I pant as I continue to rock.

"Presley! Looks like you took my advice," I hear a voice call out behind me, and Lee freezes.

"Whatever you do, don't turn around." He whispers in my ear.

So, I do exactly the opposite. I have no clue why. I just do it.

"Oh my. Presley, you weren't exaggerating. She's absolutely stunning." The woman begins to walk over. "I'm Jeanie, this horny boy's Grans."

"Um, I'm Ellie." I turn back around, waiting for Lee to help me out, since one hand is frozen on his belt buckle and the other on his shoulder.

"Grans. I'm a tad busy here." Lee just throws me a look, shrugging his shoulders.

"Seriously?" I mouth.

"Well kiddos. I guess that's my cue to leave." I hear her head for the door and open it. She whispers loudly, "Go get 'em, tiger," before leaving and shutting the door behind her.

"So—"

"That's my Grans."

"Yeah, I got that." I try to get down, but he pulls me in tighter.

"That was awkward but just know, when I let you go, you this," he motions between us, "is not over. Not by a long shot."

"I was hoping you would say that."

"I was exhausted before you got here, but suddenly, I feel as if I could go all night." He winks as we get off the desk, and he grabs my hand.

But first, we eat.

Chapter Sixteen

Lee

I can't control myself when I'm around her and the garage incident is proof of that. The moment she wrapped those legs around me is when I knew I was a goner. All reason went out the window.

I just wish I would have remembered to lock the door. Not only to give me a chance to see where things would have gone with Ellie, but to save her from the embarrassment as well.

I tried to explain that it wasn't a big deal, but with our hands up each other's shirts, it was hard to get her to see it any other way.

"Do you think she thinks I'm a slut?" Ellie blurts out as she sets the table, not even bothering to look up.

"Is that your first question?" I joke.

"I'm serious, Lee." She stops, hands on hips.

I stop plating our food and wonder what is going through her mind. Yeah, it was embarrassing for the both of us but, as awkward as it was, Grans' reaction should have given her some sense of comfort. Hell, if we would have let Grans stay, I'm pretty sure she would have cheered us on from the sidelines.

"I'm pretty sure she loves you."

"How can you tell?"

I pick up the plates and take them over the table. I'm stalling so I can come up with a logical answer, one that will put her at ease, but I'm failing miserably.

"Well, she gave me a thumbs-up." I smile at the memory.

"What?"

"Before she walked out, she gave me a thumbs-up," I mutter, turning around to grab our drinks. I take a sip of mine before placing it on the table. "Ready to eat?"

"What?"

"You ready to eat?" I walk around to her chair, pulling it out.

"No, rewind." Ellie twirls her finger in the air. "What's this about a thumbs-up?" she asks as she sits down.

"Like this." I throw my thumbs up in the air giving her my best Grans impersonation as I walk around to take a seat across from her.

"Why?"

"You are well beyond your three questions, but since we are making it up as we go, I'll give you a pass." I wink. "But just this once."

"Lee!" She laughs. "Just spit it out."

"Fine." I lay my napkin out on my lap, still continuing to take my time, before I lean in and say, "My Grans thought I was a miserable, lonely shell of a man. Overworked and tired. No time for myself."

"And?" She motions for me to hurry.

"The point is, she saw me happy." I flash her a wicked grin, one I know will drive her crazy. "Apparently being worked over isn't the same as being overworked." I wink again.

She gasps.

I laugh.

"Not funny."

"You're not a slut."

In a war of smiles, we begin a stare down. Not sure what game we are playing, but it's fun.

"You're not cute." She picks up her fork and begins to eat the casserole, then moans with pleasure.

"You sure about that?"

"Yes, but oh em gee can you cook." She quickly takes another bite.

"Thanks. My Grans taught me." I finally begin to dig in.

"Speaking of which," she says, pointing her fork toward the kitchen. "Why so much food?"

Taking another bite, I scoot my chair back and cross my legs. Picking my glass up, I take a sip before I begin. "My Grans has been diagnosed with Alzheimer's."

"Oh no." Ellie holds her hand to her chest for a moment before getting up and dragging her chair in front of me. "How bad?" she asks, leaning over, taking my hands in hers.

"Apparently, we ignored the symptoms. By the time we found out, she was in the moderate, middle stage. But lately she has shown signs of it progressing."

"I'm so sorry, Lee."

"Me too." I give her hands a squeeze. "A couple weeks ago, she was trying to boil a chicken, but forgot to add water, then went to lie down. A small fire started."

"Was anyone hurt?"

"Nope." I shake my head. "But it scared me enough to take my time in getting the kitchen put back together. So, it's only been microwavable foods and cold cuts for her."

"Oh! I take it that didn't sit well?"

"She's getting tired of it. So, until I can figure everything out, I thought I would improvise. Make a few freezer meals. Divide them up in individual proportions."

Giving my hands another squeeze, she pulls me closer. "So thoughtful," she says, leaning in and placing a soft kiss on my lips. "What are you going to do?" she asks.

"You," I reach over and tap her nose, "are at your limit." I stand and reach across the table, grabbing her plate and setting it down beside mine. "Now, eat."

"I'll remember that." Ellie sticks her tongue out while scooting her chair in.

"My turn," I say as I pull my chair in.

"I'm not sure if this is friendly dinner conversation or an interrogation," she laughs between bites.

"We can skip the dinner conversation and go straight to the friendly." I nod toward the couch.

Raising her eyebrows, she says, "I'm game."

"Let me get my round in over dinner, get this mess cleaned up and then the couch and I are all yours."

"Deal."

"So, why do you always taste like vanilla?"

She takes a drink then licks her bottom lip. "Oh, my ChapStick.

I'm obsessed."

"Why vanilla?"

"I never used to care what flavor, but my first night in Nashville, I had this gig and I always apply ChapStick before I go on. That night I had vanilla. I'm a tad superstitious, so it's now my favorite."

"Mine too," I confess, leaning in to steal a quick one. "Middle name?"

"Jane." She makes a face. "At boarding school my nickname was Plain Jane."

"You are anything but," I reply.

A little while later, I nod at her empty plate. "More?"

"Oh no, I'm so stuffed. Thank you."

"You're welcome." I collect our plates, stacking them in the sink. "Would you like to take some home with you?"

"Maybe just a little." She holds her fingers a tiny bit apart in a pinching-type gesture. "If you have enough."

"I think I went a little overboard." I purse my lips together, glancing at the mess I created.

"Possibly," she laughs, coming to stand beside me. "Where are the containers? I'll start filling them up."

"I got this. You just sit over there and relax." I nod toward the couch again.

"Tempting, but I have ulterior motives. The quicker we get this cleaned up, the sooner we will be on the couch together." She flashes me a sexy smile.

"How can I argue with that?"

"You can't." She holds her hands in the air. "So, I win! Yay!"

I think I already have.

Ellie

After the past couple days, there is one thing I know for sure. Lee loves his Grans. He would do anything for his grandmother even if it means sacrificing his own happiness.

How can you not fall for someone who loves that deeply? It's what I have always wanted. That kind of love is unconditional.

"Hey, what's going through that pretty little head of yours?" Lee says, bringing both hands up to cradle my face.

After dinner, Lee collapsed on the couch, pulling me with him, and I didn't object. But lying here, I can't help but think about my own family. Will we ever reconcile? What happens if one of them falls ill, will they even tell me? Do they even care?

I care.

"Nothing, really."

"It doesn't seem like nothing." He begins to rub slow circles on my lower back. My eyes flutter shut.

"Hey, Lee?" There is a small rap at the door before it swings open. "Mother said—"

"Dammit." He sits up, taking me with him. "Give me a minute to take care of this." Lee gives me a weak smile as he tucks my hair behind my ear.

"You were bringing dinner down, but if you are busy I'll just order a pizza," the woman continues.

"Mom, wait." He jumps over the coffee table and heads into the kitchen. He brings back a box of food.

Mom?

"I completely forgot. You got this?" He hands the food over to her.

"I can manage." She begins to turn and when she does, she does a double take.

"Oh my lord!" She sets the box down and walks over to me.

I'm a little confused. The last I knew, Lee wasn't on good terms with his mom.

"Are you any relation to Anna Clark?" She takes a couple steps forward, making me a little nervous.

"Yeah. That's my mom." I stand. "Well, now it's Anna Hawthorne."

"So she's still married to that bastard? Hmph," she mumbles, shaking her head.

"Mom!" Lee scolds. "I think it's time for you to go." He opens the door.

"Pardon me. I'm just so shocked, that's all." She looks between me and Lee. "It's just a small world."

"Mom. The food." He bends to pick it up. "You don't want to keep Grans waiting." He takes one step outside, I'm sure to get his mom to follow.

"You look just like her." She turns, shaking her head again, as she follows Lee out.

"Nice to meet you," I call after her, but Lee shuts the door, leaving me inside while they talk.

Not sure what to do, I take a seat. Waiting. A minute becomes five and five becomes ten. Laying back, I take Lee's place and settle in.

"I'm so sorry," Lee says as he opens the door.

"Really, it's okay." I begin to sit up.

"No, stay just like that." He walks around the coffee table and climbs up toward me. "Am I too heavy?"

"Not at all. I like it," I admit.

"Good. Me too." He lays his head down.

"Do you want to talk about it?" I run my fingers through his hair.

"My mom came back last night." He turns his head, resting his chin on my chest as he looks at me. His eyes are sad and for the first time, I can see the little boy behind the laugh lines and five o'clock shadow.

"And I take it you're not happy about it?"

"I don't know how to feel. She says she's back for me and to help Grans, but I can't help but wonder if there is something else." He begins to close his eyes. "That feels so good."

"Maybe I should stop?" I keep going.

"Nah. I'll be fine." Lee lays his head over my heart.

"Maybe you can just take one day at a time. Don't expect anything." I kiss the top of his head. "No expectations means no disappointments."

His chin is back on my chest and he searches my eyes. "How did you get so smart?" His lips turn up.

"Years of disappointment, I guess."

"I won't disappoint you." Lee makes a promise I'm not sure he can keep. "You know what else?" he asks, as he begins to nuzzle my neck. "This spot right here," he whispers against my skin, "was made for my kisses."

"Then by all means, kiss away." I turn my head, inviting him in to take what he wants.

And he does. Slow kisses—tender, yet demanding—as he works the spot he calls his.

Nipping.

Licking.

Sucking.

His lips follow the curve of my neck as he teases his way down to my chest. Sliding away enough material to expose the top of my breast, he places a soft kiss before he lays his head down right above my heart. "I love the way you feel against me."

"Lee—"

"Just." He inhales. "Like this." He quickly breathes out.

"Lee? You falling asleep?"

"No. Just resting my eyes." He moves a little, maybe nodding. I can't tell. "You just feel so good."

"Lee. Maybe I should—"

"Don't leave me, not ever," he pleads.

"I won't," I agree.

"Stay."

"I will."

"You promise?"

"I do."

I guess Lee isn't the only one making a promise he can't keep. The question is, who will *break* theirs first?

Chapter Seventeen

Lee

It's been five long days since I've seen Ellie. Between work, Grans and the surprise reappearance of my mom, I haven't had much time for myself.

"Hey, Scott!" Kyle hollers. "Come see me before you go."

"I just finished my rundown with the weekend crew." I head up to the site trailer. "Will now work?"

"Yeah, man. Come on in." Kyle stands there with the door propped open.

Looking over my shoulder, I search the parking lot for Drew's truck.

"Drew had to leave," Kyle says as if he's read my mind. "A slight family emergency. Something about a goat getting loose."

"They have goats now?" I question, stepping up into the trailer.

"Who knows?" He pats me on the back as I slide by. "How you doing?" Kyle points to an empty chair.

"I'm lovin' the job. I thought maybe the guys would have a hard time once you announced the promotion, but they've adjusted pretty well," I inform him as I take a seat.

I'm on edge. I thought the transition was going well, but maybe I was too preoccupied to notice any problems.

"Good, good." He nods while he digs for a folder. "But that's not why I wanted to talk to you."

"Okay?" I lean forward, ready for whatever he throws my way.

"Your grandmother, how is she doing?"

"I'm losing her, but I'm coping the best I can," I admit, for the first time, that no matter what we do, eventually the Grans I know will be gone.

"I know you have been researching memory care homes." Kyle flips through the folder until he finds the paper he has been searching for. "There it is." He turns it around and pushes it across the desk. "I want you to take a look at this."

"Lavender Springs Memory Care Home."

It's the exact same facility I've been researching for months. The only home, I feel, can give her the care she needs.

"It's top notch. The staff is the best in the Midwest," Kyle states.

"I know, I've looked into this place. But it's also forty-two hundred a month for the full time residential living. Twenty-three hundred for home care, and that only covers six-hour days."

I run the numbers in my head once again. No matter what I do, I can't afford it.

Kyle lets out a whistle. "I know. It's rough, but I have something I think will ease your mind." He reaches for the papers stacked on the printer, slapping them with a stapler before handing them over.

"I have to say, you've piqued my interest." I look through the papers.

Flipping houses?

"Not many know this, but Drew and I have been flipping houses for the past year. It was only supposed to be a one-time thing, but I had a few things I needed to take care of and Drew? Well, kids are expensive, and after the accident last year he wanted to make sure they were well taken care of. College paid for and all that stuff."

"What does this have to do with me?" I sit with the papers in my hand, trying not to jump to conclusions.

"It takes so much spare time and with Nina going to school, I don't have the time to invest in it anymore. Which is where you come in."

I scan the numbers, and everything looks great, but there is no way I can come up with the start-up.

"Kyle, I'm going to be honest. I like what I'm seeing, but I don't have the money to put into it."

"Lee, I want to be your silent partner. I put up the money, you do the work and when we make the sale I get ten percent of your profit."

"Let me get this straight. You want to front all the money, Drew and I do the work and when it sells we split it fifty, forty, ten?"

"Yeah, man." He leans back in his office chair, hands clasped behind his head. "Minus the start-up funds, of course. But you are looking at a possible one-hundred-and-seventy-five-thousand-dollar profit."

Now it's my turn to whistle. "That would pay for the first three years of Lavender Springs. More if we only did part time in the beginning."

"You in?" Kyle extends his hand.

"Hell yes!" I clasp his hand in both of mine. "Where do I sign?"

"Perfect! I'll have legal draw something up and have it to you sometime next week." He stands and comes around the desk. "We are looking to start on it in the next couple months." He slaps me on the back. "That work for you?"

"Yes, perfect. Thank you." I open the door to head out. "You coming?"

"I have a few calls to make. Then I'm out of here, but you go on."

"Kyle, thank you so much. The stress, I was…" I shake my head, thinking about the past week and how Grans has been a little irritable. Mom swears it's her declining, but Grans says my mom is being mean and I hate to say it, but this time, I'm unsure who to believe.

"I get it."

"It's gone now. Because of you."

Kyle walks over to me, placing a hand on my shoulder, looking me right in the eyes. "No, Lee. This is all you. You have worked your ass off to get here. Don't let anyone else take the credit."

Nodding, I turn and jog to my truck. Throwing my hat in the back, I hop in and grab my phone. Bringing it to life, I see a text from the exact person I want to talk to, celebrate with.

Ellie: I miss you.

Just seeing her name makes me smile. Seeing her message has me wanting to rush right over there, but first I'll settle for a quick text. I won't bother her in case she is trying to get ready with the girls.

Me: I miss you too.

Hitting send, I set the phone down as I buckle up, but my phone quickly pings.

Ellie: When are you coming over?

Me: I just need to go home and shower. I have some good news.

Ellie: Like the kind where we get to celebrate?

Me: Yup. Care to share the spotlight tonight?

Ellie: With you? Anytime. (kissy face)

Me: See you in a few.

Ellie: I can't wait! Hurry.

I throw the phone in the console and head home to shower. Tonight is a new start for many things. For me, for Grans, and hopefully for me and Ellie. Putting fears aside, I'm going in. Heart first.

Chapter Eighteen
Ellie

I can't help but run around the apartment like a crazy person. Everything I had laid out for tonight Rain nixed. Once she found out that Lee had some big news, she decided tonight needed to be "super special" to get super laid. Her words, not mine. Even though…

Ellie, get it together.

Everything was either too casual, too dressy, or too see-through. "Ugh!" I throw my hands up. "I give up!" I plop down on the bed and put my head in my hands.

"Just so you know, I'm giving you one huge eye roll right now. So huge that my eyes may just burst out of my head." Rain jumps on the bed, tackling me so I remove my hands from my face.

"Stop! You are going to mess up my hair!" I shout.

"Seriously, Ellie, dramatic much?" She jumps off the bed, landing on her feet all cat-like. "When you're nervous you catch a case of bitchatitus."

"That isn't even a word." I hop up and head to the bathroom. At least my makeup and hair look good—or they did, anyway.

"Sure it is. Urban Dictionary says so." Rain gets out her phone, swiping it alive. "Bitchatitus—Having or contracting the illness of being a bitch."

"You really think I'm being a bitch?" I peek my head out of the bathroom, straightener in one hand and toothbrush in the other.

"Nah, you're just getting a little high-strung, which is really abnormal for you. So, what's going on?" Rain starts flipping through my closet. "This is more than just Lee having some news."

Standing in the bathroom, I finish brushing my teeth and think about her words. Spitting, I walk out to where she is. "Last time I played, he left. Walked out without even saying good-bye." I reach in the closet and pull out my favorite dark, ripped jeans. As I slide them on, I say, "What if he leaves again?"

"Have you ever asked him why he left?"

I shake my head no.

"Why haven't you?" Rain asks the very question I have asked myself a million times.

Why?

I had the chance when we were playing Three Questions, but after he told me about his grandmother, I thought maybe that was the reason. Maybe there was an emergency and he had to go. Then again, maybe not.

"Scared to find out the answer, I guess," I admit, reaching past her to pull out a black-and-white striped tank.

"Oh! I see where you're going with this." Rain ignores my admission and begins to go through my shirts, pulling out a white tank. Then she moves over to my jewelry box and pulls out three necklaces and two blinged-out leather wraps. "Pair those with that and then the red high heel booties with a matching lip and you are set."

"You don't think I need to wear a dress?" I question her advice.

"No! Do you want everyone in the crowd to get a peep show while you're performing?" Rain flips up her skirt, exposing her thong, and continues. "In case you forgot, it's not that type of stage." She winks.

"Seriously, you're messed up."

"I know. I blame my parents and all the drugs." Rain heads into the kitchen. "Wanna do a shot before we go down?"

"They didn't do drugs back then," I say, nodding my head in approval at the alcohol.

"Well, still. I blame them for everything. It's my excuse for therapy." She downs her shot and mine, before she pours two more. "And it will still be my excuse when my kids are in therapy." She laughs.

"I don't even know what to say right now," I respond as I sit down on the couch to put on my booties. These aren't the most comfortable, but they're definitely the cutest.

"Nothing. You say nothing." She hands me a shot. "To new beginnings?"

"Yes, to new beginnings." We clink our glasses together. "And staying," I get in quickly before I let the alcohol burn its way into my system.

"Speaking of which." She picks up my phone and hands it to me. "Lover boy is texting."

Grabbing the phone from her hands, I swipe it alive.

Lee: Downstairs. You want me to come up?

Quickly, I type out a reply.

Me: We are just finishing up. Be down in five minutes.

Lee: See you soon.

His message causes me to get a tad excited. "He's here!" I jump up and quickly pick up some things around the room just in case he wants to visit afterward.

"Interesting." Rain leans against the counter.

"What?"

"Just think." She crosses her arms. "If our parents would have let us have boys up to our rooms, we probably would have kept them clean."

With a bra in one hand and a wet towel in the other, I shrug and toss everything in a basket. Rooms may have been clean, but I'm pretty sure the pregnancy rate would have gone up.

"El, your phone is BLOW-ING UP over there."

Typing in my passcode. I see it's Lee.

Lee: Jen just walked in.

Oh good!

Lee: Jake's brother's here.

Oh shit!

Me: Is he alone?

Lee: That was Jen. She took my phone.

Lee: She has grabby hands.

Me: Wait, how grabby?

Lee: Just the phone.

Me: Good.

Lee: You jealous?

Me: Just a little...

Me: Not like hunt you down and slash your tires jealous.

Lee: I get it, but YOU have nothing to worry about.

Me: You make me smile.

Lee: Ditto.

Locking the phone, I hold it to my chest and sigh before I slide it in my back pocket.

"Loverboy?" Rain purrs.

I turn to face Rain and break the news I know she doesn't want to hear. "Jordan is here."

"Son of a bitch!" She slams her glass down.

She turns around, pours a double and downs it before I can say anything else.

"Rain?"

Ignoring me, she goes through her usual routine. Money and lipstick in bra, ID in one pocket and cell in the other. "You ready?"

"Yeah." I pack up my guitar and grab a couple of the picks Rain brought over the other day.

"Good cause this place is about to get lit!" She bounces out the door.

I'm not sure what is going on but seeing her like this isn't good. Rain with a copious amount of liquor is unpredictable.

"Not too lit. Right? 'Cause I have this performance." I follow Rain down the stairs, nonchalantly reminding her.

"Of course! Tonight is going to be off the hook!" she shouts back.

"Rain?" I run past her, blocking the door. "Just remember he didn't deserve you."

"El." She reaches for the handle, pulling open the door, not giving me a choice but to move. "Don't worry about me." She nods to the bar. "See that guy over there? Tonight is about new beginnings and getting laid."

"I'm pretty sure we said new beginnings and staying."

"I'm thinking getting laid sounds better. So, run over there to your man and get you a piece." She winks while pushing me toward the bar. "Lee! Come get your girl," she shouts, causing Lee and everyone else in the bar to look in my direction.

"I'd be happy to." Lee hops off the stool and comes over to me, pulling me into his arms, whispering into the sweet spot that was made just for him. "Hi."

It's crazy how one simple word, one little gesture, can say so much.

Hi—*I missed you.*

Hi—*You look amazing.*

Hi—*I can't wait till we are alone.*

Hi—*Don't be nervous.*

Hi—*Let's have some fun.*

One word said everything it needed to say for me to know tonight is going to be one to remember.

Lee

Tonight is something I never knew I was missing. I wasn't forced to grow up faster than I wanted. I chose to. The need to give back to the people who loved me unconditionally was greater than a drunken frat party or an unnecessary relationship.

Maybe even a few were one-night stands. Well, okay maybe a lot of them, but it's not because they weren't nice girls; most of them were and maybe even were girlfriend material. I just felt given the choices I made, nothing more than one night would work.

Then I met Ellie. Being with her is definitely more than necessary. Ellie Thorne flipped my world upside down and I've been happy hanging here ever since.

"So, are you going to tell me the good news?" Ellie, leans into me, her mouth a soft tickle on my ear. "'Cause I'm dying to know."

Reaching my arm out, I wrap it around Ellie's shoulder, pulling her close. "You know that promotion I told you about?"

"Yeah?" she says with excitement.

"No—no, but I guess they were so pleased with my progress they decided to make me an offer I couldn't refuse." I stand and hold out my hand.

"Where are we going?" She seems confused.

"Yeah! Where you going, Scott?" Jen asks loudly.

"I bet…" Rain leans over and whispers in Jen's ear.

"Ohhhhh!" Jen winks. Then they both get up and head toward the spotlights.

Gavin, who manages Spotlight, gave the girls a few tokens to run the spotlights free of charge, and since this Jordan guy is down on the dance floor with the slut of the month or whatever Rain called her, I'm sure they will be preoccupied for a while.

"Never mind." I sit down, pulling her with me, tucking us away in the corner of the high-back lounger.

"I could get used to this." She snuggles into me.

"Well, hopefully, with this new project we will be able to do this more often because last week killed me." I pull her closer, placing a light kiss against her temple.

"And..." Ellie reaches between us and tickles my side.

"Oh yeah." I throw my head back. "They asked me to go in on a project that will be extremely profitable."

"Doing what?" Ellie hangs on to my every word.

"Flipping a house that had been foreclosed on." I sit up so I can look her in the eyes and take her hands in mine. "Ellie, this will give me the money I need to support my Grans."

"Really? For Lavender Springs?" Her voice is hopeful.

Ellie and I spent hours talking while she was over at my house, then spent the morning playing our little game until I brought her home. She paid attention to everything I said, down to the name of the care center I was researching.

"Yeah. It may be the end of the year before I get the money, but Mom..." I tighten my lips. Just saying her name still seems like a foreign word. "Now that she is back, she's been helping out more. The question is for how long?"

Placing a hand on either side of my face, Ellie pulls me close, taking a kiss, and giving me reassurance.

Pulling back, she searches my eyes. "I know you're worried, but your Grans wants you to live your life for you."

"I know. That's what makes it so hard. How can I live a life she wants me to live when I'm fighting so damn hard for her to remember hers?" I close my eyes, tilting my head back.

"Hey, look at me."

I do.

"With your mom in the picture and this new opportunity, it gives you the ability to do both." She smiles.

"You won't hear me complaining about that. I still have a lot of you I want to discover. Every. Single. Inch of you." I pull her into my arms and nuzzle her neck, my new favorite place.

"I like the sound of that." Ellie snakes her hands up my back and into my hair, whispering, "Sometimes, all we can do is take a chance, and you're mine."

And I want more than anything for you to be mine.

Chapter Nineteen

Lee

Eloise Hawthorne—Ellie Thorne, the same girl. Who knew I would fall for the girl from the other side of the tracks. The more prominent, rolling in money, side of the tracks. One where lives were carefully constructed, and futures mapped out. Ellie is everything I never wanted. She stands for a life I have run from but am now sprinting toward. She is searching for a future I constantly try to bury. Yet, here we are. Writing, erasing and marking it all back up again.

"You and me." Rain comes toward me. "Dance now." She pulls me up, but I sit right back down.

My plans for the rest of the night are to watch Ellie on stage. Tonight is big for her and I want to make sure she knows I'm here, watching.

"Come on. Jordan is out there and Jake is behind the bar and, well…" She yanks me back up. "I don't have time to give you my history. The point is, it's fucked-up. So, I'm calling in a favor from my best friend's boyfriend. Dance with me."

"Fine. No twerking or whatever it is you have been doing with that thing."

She rolls her eyes. "It's called working it and you're just jelly that you don't have all this." She turns around and does this little thing with her ass, causing me to fall forward laughing.

Catching my breath, I follow her out to the dance floor. "Just know the *only* reason I'm going out there is to be closer to the stage. To Ellie."

"I get it, Lover Boy. Don't make this more than what it is." She pulls us down the two levels of stairs and across the dance floor until we are practically next to the stage.

"Nice spot!" I try to move toward the music.

"Don't talk." She moves around me in a circle. "I'm trying to figure out where they went." She raises her voice, trying to be heard above the pulsating beat.

"Have you thought about just talking to him?" I shout.

"Yes! Just a million times." She comes to stand in front of me. "Look, I'm trying to get someone's attention. So, I'm going to turn around and back it up on you. Act like you enjoy it. Hell, look at the stage and play Where is Ellie. You know, like Waldo?" She swivels around and does exactly what she promised. "Remember, enjoy it." Rain reminds me, hollering over her shoulder.

Scanning around the stage area, I finally see Ellie. "Rain, I don't think Ellie would—"

Not a fucking chance.

Not giving Rain even a second thought I push through the small crowd blocking me from the one person who needs my help the most right now.

Some drunk guy is standing behind her, hands all over her as she tries to get ready for her set. Ellie is trying to push him off, but he keeps coming back.

"I have a horn you can blow." The drunk fuck tries to flirt or whatever he thinks he's doing.

"Cheesy pickup lines are my thing." I grab the guy by the collar and pull him off. "When a girl says no, you fucking listen." I throw him down to the side. "Don't fucking touch her or anyone else tonight," I seethe.

"I thought I told you to never come back." A deep voice barrels toward us. "Out! Now!" He swoops the drunk up by doing some kind of death grip to his neck where he instantly rises. "Sorry, Ellie." He gives her an apologetic look and leaves.

"Who's that?" I point my thumb toward the exit.

"Shapiro, the bouncer." She watches them leave then turns around.

"You okay?" I place a hand on her shoulder and wait for her to acknowledge me, but she doesn't.

"I'm not. What you did," she twists around, "Was—"

"Saving you?" I point out.

"I don't need saving." She pulls the strap over her head.

"Hey, where is this coming from?" I pull her in and envelop her in my arms. Her tension begins to deflate.

"I don't know. I guess I'm just nervous," she confesses.

"I thought you don't get nervous."

"I normally don't, but tonight is different."

"Different is good." I lean down, kissing her on the top of the head. "You better?"

She nods.

"Good, me too." I turn her around in my arms and give her a little push to the stage. "You're up."

"Watch me?"

"Of course." I wink and turn to find a spot close to the stage when she comes over the speakers.

"Hey y'all. Let's give it up for our favorite Nashville girl, Myles Davis." she works the crowd, continuing, "I'm Ellie Thorne and who is here looking for a little *trouble*? I heard this is the place to come to," she says into the mic, slow and confident, while the audience is bursting with excitement. "You ready for what I got?" She strums chords of the song, a song I know all too well.

Breathe.

The walls are closing in. Everywhere I look, walls of people.

Breathe.

Pushing my way through one person at a time.

Breathe.

"Lee, you okay?" Someone calls after me.

Breathe.

Hands on my knees, I try to catch my breath.

Breathe.

I hear someone behind me.

Everything is muffled.

The voice.

The music.

Her.

It's just *words*. I tell myself. *Words* my mother listened to. *Words* sung by a beautiful, caring and supportive girl. *Words* that mean nothing.

But Ellie, she means something. She deserves a chance. The same chance she has encouraged me to take.

Pushing back the demons, I turn around and take a single step toward the stage. Fighting the war within, I take another step and then another. Keeping my eyes on Ellie.

My strength.

My choice.

My chance.

So, I stand here. In the front row, looking up to the girl who inspires me to be more. Watching her every move, listening to every word, laughing at every joke.

I stay.

Ellie Thorne not only owns the stage, she owns my heart.

Chapter Twenty
Ellie

Tonight was amazing. The best performance I have ever had, and it is because of Lee. I got up there to play for him. To sing the words I'm too afraid to say. Then when I saw him standing there in the front row, every word became clearer, the notes longer, the beat louder.

Lee Scott, my muse. The man who is right behind this very door. Waiting for me.

Me.

All because I asked him to stay.

Unlocking the door, I push it open, unsure of what I'm walking into to.

"Lee?" I call tentatively.

"Hey, you." He comes around the corner, skidding to a stop when he sees me. "Damn, girl. On a scale of one to ten you are definitely a nine, and I'm the one you need."

I can't help but giggle. His little pickup lines, as cheesy as they are, are one of the many things I look forward to with Lee Scott.

"You are something else." I close the distance between us.

"Yeah?"

"Yeah!" I nod.

"Come here." He reaches around, pulling me close. "You were absolutely amazing tonight."

Hiding my face in his chest I thank him, but even though tonight was one of the greatest nights of my life, I can't help but replay the moment I thought he was leaving again.

He walked out on that song in the coffee bar and he almost walked out tonight.

How can someone who keeps running from me stay?

I'm so confused.

He planned on staying. I see that he's showered and in a pair of shorts, which means he wanted to stay.

"Lee?"

"Yeah?" He lets me go and heads into the kitchen, where he starts opening cabinets. "You want some tea?"

"Tea's good, but I need to talk to you."

"Okay?" He opens a couple more doors, looking for what he needs.

"Stop!"

"What?" He turns around with a mug he finally found in one of the cabinets.

I walk over to him, take the cup out of his hands and place it on the counter. "Why did you leave?"

"I didn't." He seems confused. "I stayed."

"I saw you walk away."

Rubbing his face, he leans his head back. "You did."

"Why?" I take a step closer and reach out to touch his face, but he stops me, holding my hand in his. "You walked away the first night and again tonight. I was playing the same song."

"Fuck." He sighs. "My situation is so damn messed up. I'm not sure if you will want to stay after you hear all my fucked-upness."

"Try me."

"My mom was obsessed with Elvis." He points to himself. "Presley Aaron Scott—which I don't let anyone call me but—"

"Grans," we say in unison.

"Right." He continues. "When my mom left I was seven, I hated her. I went two years before I realized she wasn't coming back and that was when I started going by Lee and refused to listen to anything by Elvis." He takes me by the hand and pulls me to the bed. "I despised my mom's career choice. I thought all of you guys were the same, always looking for the next big thing."

"We aren't all the same." I roll over on top of him so that he'll listen to what I'm saying this time. "I will not leave."

"Don't." He carefully rolls me off and stands up. "You can't promise that."

"I can," I dispute, sitting up.

"You are so much more than Spotlight. I saw it tonight," Lee says, leaning against the wall across from the bed.

"I wouldn't go that far." I blush

"I *know* you are. I believe in you."

"If you believe in me then believe me when I say I'm not going anywhere."

"Ellie, my mom left because she fooled herself into thinking she was *someone*. She lived a lie, but you? You are the real deal, living the truth." He tilts his head back, pushing himself off the wall. "I can't let you stay."

"Don't!" I exclaim, moving in front of him. "You don't get to tell me what I'm going to do. Maybe this," I wave my hands around, "is enough for me. Maybe you are enough."

"Being enough isn't always enough to stay. You do realize that, right?"

"First my parents and now you." I begin to pace. "All I've ever wanted is someone to believe in me enough to support me. To protect me." I stop in front of him. "My parents failed me and now you."

"I do believe in you, I do support you. And now I'm protecting you from a life of regret. Which is what you'll have if you stay."

"Bullshit. You are protecting yourself."

"Ellie," he pleads. "Just—"

"What happened to taking chances, Lee?" I walk past him and head to the bathroom but turn around to give him something to think about. "Maybe I will leave, but that doesn't mean this," I reach up and rub my chest over my heart, "doesn't stay."

"You don't see it now—"

"I'm going to take a shower." I cut him off. "And you can choose to leave if you want to, but I'm asking you to stay. I need you to stay. Because just like you have your demons, I have mine. So please don't leave me."

"Okay," he agrees.

"Okay."

I head to the bathroom to take a shower and give him the time he needs to let this all soak in.

I am not going anywhere. What Lee doesn't understand is, I never had a reason to stay.

Until now—Presley Aaron Scott.

Lee

Every moment I'm with her she plays on my heart strings, strumming the chords of a song I desperately want her to sing.

Play me.

I've been so careful to not let our worlds collide. I've kept a protective barrier up, but I can't help but want to break it back down, busting through the walls to expose what could be.

Us.

I need her, but taking Ellie would only be selfish, sealing our hearts to a disastrous fate. And as much as I want to worship *every single inch* of her body, I can't. I won't. It would destroy us both.

So, I lay here, because she asked me for the one thing I couldn't deny her.

To stay.

Stay and be the man she needs to me to be.

Support *her.*

Protect *her.*

Don't leave *her.*

Even if it destroys me, I will give her this. Not only because she has never felt any of these things, but because I haven't either, and just for once, I'm going to throw all hopes and fears out the window and hold on. Even if it's just for one night.

Rolling over to my side. I watch the girl who flipped my world upside down with one little swivel of a stool. Padding across the room in her barely there boy shorts and tiny tank she leaves nothing to the imagination.

With each step closer, I find my resolve slipping. The spark within igniting the flame. Her smile, the fuel.

"Hey." Her voice is quiet, but the underlying meaning is heard loud and clear.

"Hi," I say as I pull back the covers and she begins to climb in.

She's lying on her back, and I know she is wondering what will happen next, but I told her, warned her, *nothing* could.

Nothing.

I say the word over again in my head, reminding myself of the reasons why, but now I'm wondering if it's the *right* thing to do or am I just running from the truth?

"Look at me."

She rolls over to face me, her mouth calling to *me*. Her body screaming for *me*.

For me.

One taste—one kiss to punish my memory.

Reaching out, I lift her chin and whisper the promise across her lips. "I'm here."

"You are," she agrees, breathing life I didn't know I lost back into me. Closing my eyes, I inhale all she has to give. "Kiss me." And I do.

Soft, slow, demanding—a kiss meant to be remembered. A kiss that catches me in a moment of weakness.

I need more.

My tongue traces the seam of her lips, swallowing the moan that escapes. The only invitation I need to keep going.

Urgent.

Desperate.

My thumbs brush her cheeks but it's not enough. Flipping my calloused palm over, I run the back of my hand down her neck, over her shoulder, down her body. Imprinting every curve to memory. Never to be forgotten.

"Ellie," I groan her name, asking her to tempt me for more.

"Please," she begs, rolling over on her back, inviting me to take what I promised myself I wouldn't.

"Ellie," I growl as I begin to seduce her.

Climbing on top of her, I kiss, lick, nip my way to where I shouldn't be.

Just one taste, I tell myself.

My hand moves lower, dragging her shorts down while she pulls her tank up. Looking up at her, I wait for her to stop me, because in this moment I can't. Being with her, all control is thrown out the window.

Keeping my eyes on Ellie's, I take it.

One lick.

One swipe.

One taste.

But it's not enough. Her moan is a siren's call, taking me under.

As I slide one finger in, she falls back, losing all control. Her movements are wild, abandoned. Then two. Twisting, pumping, giving her what she wants.

A few more licks and a swipe, her hands fly to my hair.

Tugging.

Pulling.

It doesn't take long before I can taste the tidal wave of pleasure that crashes through her. I lap it up greedily, humming my approval. I lick her until she screams out my name.

I shouldn't have done it, but as soon as our lips met, I knew she wanted it.

I needed it.

Placing tender kisses up one thigh and down the other, I wait as her body works its way back down.

"Presley, I need you." Her voice is strained, tired.

Shaking my head, I follow my path upward. Pulling her shorts up and her shirt down as I go.

"I just want—"

"I need you, like this," I confess, lying beside her, pulling her close. Ellie's back to my front we just lie here.

The song is over.

She sleeps.

Chapter Twenty-One
Ellie

"Ellie." I hear Lee beside me, but not next to me. "Ellie, I have to go," Lee whispers as he brushes hair out of my face.

"No you don't. Leaving is a choice, Lee. I thought we discussed this." I open my eyes, expecting to see his sexy-as-sin smile.

Wrong.

"Ellie." Lee stands.

"I'm sorry, Lee. I'm an asshole in the mornings. They aren't my thing. I thought I was being cute trying to get you to stay." I pat the empty side of the bed. "It's cold. I'm cold. Heat me up," I blurt out, unsure of what I'm saying because mornings suck and apparently, I do too.

"I wish I could, but I really need to check on Grans," he says before bending over and stealing a lingering kiss.

"You brushed your teeth?"

"I came prepared." He winks.

"But I didn't." I hold my hand up to my mouth and breathe out.

"Don't worry. I held my breath."

"Shut it." I reach over, pick up the first pillow I can find and chuck it in his direction.

"Do you care if I make a cup of coffee to go?" Lee asks but is already in the kitchen pulling out mugs and fixing the coffee before I answer.

"Not if you make me one too." I climb out of the bed and sneak up behind him. "You know, if you were coffee grounds," I whisper as I wrap my arms around his waist, resting my head on his back, "you would be espresso because you are so damn fine."

His laugh vibrates through me. "That's a good one. Here." Lee hands me a mug while he twists the lid on his.

"Good enough for you to stay?" I pad over to the freezer, dropping a couple ice cubes into my coffee to cool it.

"I really need to go. Even though I'm trying really hard to have faith in my mom, I need to see for myself that Grans is okay." Lee only has to take a couple steps to the door. "Call you later?" He opens the door. "Kiss me."

Closing the distance, I rise up on my tiptoes and bare my neck. "Morning breath."

"Uh-huh. I think you're trying to tempt me." He leans in, placing a soft kiss on his spot. "Dammit." He drops his bag, puts down his coffee and lifts me into his arms.

"It worked." I smile and he turns us so that my back is against the wall.

His kisses are slow and needy as he works his way up the curve of my neck. "It did." He nips at my ear before he lets me fall slowly down his body.

"I really have to go." Lee gives me a look of regret. "Next time I'll make sure this is taken care of."

"I get it." I follow him out. "Call me later?"

"Of course." He throws his bag over his shoulder and rounds the corner.

Just as I'm about to head back inside I see the girl from the other day carrying a basket of something that smells delicious.

"Whatcha got there?" I ask just as my stomach lets out a big growl.

Nothing.

What is it with this girl? "I promise I'm not the big bad wolf ready to take your basket of goodies. Although this thing here," I point to my growling stomach, "says to knock you down and take the muffins and run."

Her eyes are wide. She hurries inside and quickly locks the door. My apartment only has two basic locks. Deadbolt and the one on the doorknob. But every time Shapiro leaves I can hear his girlfriend or whoever lock up at least three more bolts. Which is really weird because there is already one lock and one keypad on the outside of the door.

I go back inside and debate: Do I fix myself something for breakfast, climb back into bed, or accept it is morning and start my day by actually getting ready?

Looking over at the bed, I swear it's calling out to me. "Pick me. Choose me. Sleep on me." How can I say no to that?

Giving in to the oversized pillowtop perfection, I make my way over there, but just as I'm getting ready to climb back in I hear a knock at the door.

Muffins!

Maybe she felt sorry for me. And if not me, maybe my belly. Running over to the door in hopes of all things lemon poppy seed, I swing it open, but instead of seeing my neighbor, Myles is standing there with some guy who has his back turned, talking on his cell.

"Myles? I thought you went back last night?" I close the door a little, peeking my head around. I'm suddenly feeling a little underdressed.

"I was going to, but…" She nods toward me. "How about you change and then we all can talk."

"Talk?"

"Don't ask questions. We have to be at the airport in three hours and it takes one to get there."

"Okay. Give me one minute." I shut the door and rush around to get ready.

Tossing on an oversized sweatshirt and last night's jeans, I hurry and brush my teeth. Grabbing a hair tie, I secure my hair in a messy bun just as I reach the door and open it.

"It's about time," Myles jokes and pushes her way past me. The guy with a way-too-serious look, who is still on the phone, follows. "Ellie, I would like you to meet Jagger Richards." She gestures at his hand. "Jagger, meet Ellie Thorne."

"*The* Jagger Richards?" I take his hand, giving it an overly eager shake.

"Yeah, I'm him." He swings his leather bag off his shoulder, setting it on the table. "I'm going to make this quick. As Myles just told you, we have a flight to catch." He flips through some papers. "Here they are." He hands me a thick envelope.

"What's this?" I take it from his hands.

"It's a contract."

"A contract?" I can't believe what I'm hearing.

"Ellie, you're going to Nashville!" Myles screams.

"Nashville?" I'm in disbelief.

"Listen, I don't have time to go through all the details but…shit!" he exclaims as he pulls out his phone again. "I'm sorry, I have to take this.

"Ellie, it's everything we ever talked about." Myles is standing in front of me, both hands clasped on my shoulders. "Your dreams are coming true."

"Yeah."

"Why don't you seem more excited?" She scrunches her brows, confused, I'm sure, by my lack of freaking out. Nashville was a dream of mine. It was where I was going to find my freedom, my escape from all the expectations.

"I am, it's just—"

"I'm sorry about that. Myles, we have to go," he demands as he slides the phone back in his pocket. "Ellie, look over the contract and give me a call by next week."

"You'll need a lawyer too." Myles winks.

Jagger shoots her a look.

"My card is in there. I'll be expecting to hear from you sooner rather than later. Have a great day!"

"See you soon!" Myles waves and just as quick as they were here they are gone, leaving me standing here in the middle of my loft apartment, struggling with what I want.

Before Lee, Nashville was my one and only dream. After Lee, I want more. Crave more. Something I'm not sure Nashville could give me.

If I left now, would I be running? Would I be doing the exact same thing I accused Lee of doing?

If I *stay*, will it be enough?

Lee

In a perfect world, I would have been able to stay. To hold her, love on her, show her how much I need her in my life. But my world is far from perfect. It's chaotic and unpredictable. It's everything she doesn't deserve.

Ellie, she deserves to have everything she has ever dreamed of. Unlike me, who had the love of two grandparents, she's had two parents who cared more about themselves than about their only child—a beautiful, talented woman who is destined for great things. Dreams be damned, she will make it her reality.

My reality is far from wonderful, but it's the hand I've been dealt and I'm playing it the best I can.

I've walked up this same path more times than I can remember, but today it feels different. With Grans you always knew what to expect, but now…I hang my head as I reach the door. The house which once was a home is now a building of foreign memories.

Pulling the storm door open, I walk in, the same as I do every day.

"Katie?" I call out.

"There you are. Did you have a good night?" She gathers her things she had set on the counter. I'm sure she's been counting down the minutes till she can get home.

"It was." I look around for Grans. "Where is she?"

"She's lying down. Lee, there is something I think you should know." I can tell from Katie's eyes she's beginning to worry.

I reach out and grab hold of the counter, bracing myself for whatever bad news she's throwing my way but when I do, my hand slips and papers go flying everywhere.

"Well shit." I squat down and gather the loose pages and straighten them on the counter. "I'm not sure if I got them back in order." I quickly flip, through double-checking the page numbers when I see my grandmother's name. "Katie?" I narrow my eyes, quickly going through the rest of the document.

This can't be.

"Lee, that's what I wanted to talk to you about. Your mom—" she tries to explain the situation, but the moment I hear my mom's name. I lose it.

Waving the papers in the air, I demand, "My mom did this?"

"Yes, but—"

"What's going on in here?" My mom swings the door open. "Oh! Hey, Presley."

"Lee!" I seethe. "Why don't *you* tell *me*?" I throw the papers down on the table. "Selling the house?"

"I better get going." Katie squeezes my arm. "It's going to be okay," she whispers as she gives my back a little pat on her way out.

"You have no right!" I quickly turn to go face-to-face with the woman who has never been here but is suddenly back.

"I do." She watches me.

"The hell if you do." I begin to pace, hands behind my head. "You left and I don't care if you had a fucking drug problem or not. This house is more than a piece of property. It's my home and I'll be damned if you're going to waltz in here after years of taking everything from her and take more."

"Are you done?"

"Hell no, I'm not done! That woman is everything to me. She was my mom when you weren't there. Fuck!" I run my hands through my hair. "She *is* my mom. She hugged me when I missed you. Kissed my tears away when I cried for you. She prayed with me when I had nightmares. She supported me when I was ready to give up. She made me the man I am now."

She nods, taking everything I'm throwing at her.

"Nothing to say? All out of excuses?" I spit out.

"This was just to get an appraisal of what the house would be worth. Your grandmother put the house in your name. You are the only one who can put this house on the market and I thought, since you have had to handle all this on your own, that I could help you out, because that is why I'm here. To help." She rips the papers up, tossing them in the trash before she continues. "She knew she needed help and she didn't want to burden you."

"She isn't a burden," I whisper.

"No, but she needs help. More than what we can give her." She digs in her purse and pulls out a few pamphlets. "I know it's hard to talk about it. It's not easy for me either—"

"What are those?" I choose to ignore the *we* part.

"I found a care center that is affordable, but the house needs to go—"

"I don't give a damn about affordable, I want the best care," I interrupt.

"Listen, the house is in your name. Only you can make the decision to sell it, but I have power of attorney. Which means—"

I start trembling. "Excuse me?"

"Three months ago your grandmother hired a lawyer to get everything lined up before she couldn't do it herself. He suggested she give someone power of attorney. That is when she called me."

I can't believe what I'm hearing. "Why you?"

"Because she didn't want you to have to deal with it," she tells me.

Something doesn't make sense. The house, power of attorney, my mom coming back after all these years. Then it's like a light bulb goes off.

"I get it now! You were hoping I would agree to sell the house so Grans could get the care she needs and you can run away again, draining her of everything she had left."

I'm fuming. She has been nothing but a druggy whore looking for big break and now she is going to come into my home and strip it bare of memories.

I yank her purse out of her hands and toss it out the door. "Just go!" I walk down the hall and head to my old room where she is staying. "Get your things and go." I reach into the closet and throw her suitcase on the bed and throw clothes in, one drawer at a time. "You are not welcome here anymore."

"Lee!" my mom cries. "Please don't do this. I was only trying to help. Your Grans asked me to."

"Oh! Because some old lady who is losing her mind asks you to help, you come running back. Come on. You don't give a fuck about her."

"Lee!" Grans hollers from behind us. "Get out of my house," she shouts.

"Grans," I turn around, pleading. "I didn't mean it."

"Out!" she screams. "I want you out and don't come back."

"Grans, please," I beg.

"Sammy-Jo, how many times have I told you about having boys in your room?"

"Grans, it's me. Presley." I take a step toward her, but my mom holds me back, shaking her head.

"Mother, he was just going." She looks at me, signaling for me to leave, but how can I?

"He better, before your dad gets home." Grans' eyes move from Mom to me. "You. Don't belong here."

I glance between my mom and Grans, wondering how this even happened. How did things start to go downhill so fast?

"Lee, just go. This isn't her right now. I'll take care of it." Mom tries to comfort me.

Too late.

Too late to *help*.

Too late to be *strong*.

Too late to take back the *words*.

Chapter Twenty-Two

Lee

At twenty-four I never expected to make a life-changing decision like this. Getting married, changing jobs, buying a house? Sure. But this? Hell no! This decision, as selfish as it could be, shouldn't be that at all. I need to make the best one for her. For Grans.

The need to keep holding on shouldn't outweigh her need for proper care. Right now we are managing, but her bad days are outweighing the good and as much as I don't want to do it, I have to make a decision—sooner rather than later.

Which puts me in another bind. Do I go ahead and refinance the house to pay for Lavender Springs partial home care or do I wait? Keep up this exhausting routine I've set for us all?

Not only does my decision affect Grans, it affects every single person who helps her daily. How long can I keep calling in favors? How long is too long to ask someone to basically give up their whole week to care for a woman who is losing who she is? Each and every day is a gamble of what to expect.

So, I do it. I do what my financial resources will allow by getting her the proper care she deserves. I fill out the application, have my mom sign and seal Grans' fate. Maybe with having the trained staff stopping by we can keep Grans around longer.

By finally moving forward you would think I would feel some sort of relief, but I don't. I tried to prepare myself. I planned for this exact moment, searching for ways to build income to give her the best care. But, now that she actually needs it, why do I feel like shit? Why does it feel like I'm giving up?

Betraying my promise. My word.

Ellie

Today is one of those days when I'm not sure what I'm doing. I'm doubting every decision I make.

Is it for me or for someone else?

Am I content, or do I need more?

Music was my everything, my outlet from everyday life. And now, I'm not even sure if I'm playing for me anymore or if I'm playing just to prove *them* wrong.

I sang to get attention, to be heard, to be accepted. I sang like my life depended on it and then I was singing to spend my nights alone.

Then Presley Aaron Scott came crashing into my life and changed everything. I was no longer singing for a job, for a place to live or to punish the people who abandoned me. I played because I needed it. He tuned my life into a perfect song.

He's my melody.

I don't need anything else. I just need him.

But singing shouldn't be about someone else. If I can't learn to sing for myself, then why am I even performing at all?

Sitting down on the floor, I pull out my guitar, hugging it to my chest. Music has never left me alone.

I close my eyes, let myself go, and begin to play. I feel every high, every low. Every fear, every joy. Every pain, every scar.

I let myself feel, for me.

With each chord I play, the answer becomes more clear. My songs become wishes, but only I can make them come true. I know this now.

Tears fall, not because I'm sad, but because I know the answer. It's time I bet my life on me.

Wiping away the tears, I gently set the guitar back in the case and begin to close the lid when a folded piece of stationary falls out.

Lee.

My hands, eager. My heart, pounding. I open it to see what he has to say.

Ellie Jane –

I'm sorry. I am so, so sorry that I didn't stick up for you. I'm sorry for each and every time you stood up and I watched you get knocked back down and did nothing. I should have been stronger, like you.

You see, from the moment you were conceived I knew you were destined for great things. You, my little angel, were a fighter. ARE A FIGHTER. You kicked and sang your way into this world. That's right. You didn't cry, you sang. The greatest song anyone could have given me.

I tried to be your voice when you didn't have one, and reason when he wouldn't listen. I thought we had won. The piano lessons were supposed to be a start. Instead, he saw what I saw and got scared.

When he loves, it's fierce. It's what made me fall for him in the first place. You see, the more your talent would shine, the angrier he became. You were like me and he desperately wanted you to be like him. You being like me meant he had to fight harder. And deep down, I think he knew it was a losing battle. Keeping me was easy. As much as I wanted a career, I wanted a family more. I don't consider it me giving in. I call it a win. My family is my prize.

Ellie Jane, your father loves you the best way he knows how. I'm not asking you to come back. As much as I want you here, you're bigger than this. You are special and the whole world should see what I know you to be.

So, my angel, fly away, soar through the skies. Be you.

Love,

Mom

When I walked out those doors, I wanted my mom. I wanted her to comfort me, to tell me everything was going to be okay. She didn't. She watched me go, but these words came when I needed them the most. I know now that leaving was easy, but the scariest part is letting go.

Thank you, Mom.

Chapter Twenty-Three

Lee

Thank God for an early weekend. Drew gave me lead on a project and by changing up a few things we were able to complete the tasks early for the week, giving us all an extra day off. It makes me look good and saves WilliamSon Construction a ton of money in the process. It's a win-win.

After a quick shower and packing a bag, my weekend of surprises is set in motion. A weekend that I know Ellie and I both need. After multiple failed attempts to meet up this week, we finally gave up.

So here I am, standing in front of her door, waiting.

"Lee!" She swings it open.

"Hey, I know you're busy today, but I was wondering if you would add me to your to-do list?" I wink, giving her a quick peck as I walk past.

"That one was bad." Ellie laughs.

"I'm going to disagree." I turn around. "It got your attention, didn't it?" I reach out and wrap an arm around her lower back, pulling her close. "Let me kiss you."

"I'm all yours." She tilts her head to the side, causing me to smile.

"You like this?" I place a tender kiss in a spot I know drives her wild.

"Uh huh." She lets out a sigh as she closes her eyes, relaxing into my arms.

I give her a quick nip and she screeches. "What did you do that for?"

"Waking you up, El." I tickle her side as she jumps away.

"Trust me. I was awake." She slides her way back into my arms and looks up through her lashes, her hazel eyes shining with desire.

"You're killing me," I admit. My self-control slowly fading.

"It's been days. I would say you are the one killing me—slowly. Especially with all these secrets." Ellie reaches up, placing a quick kiss on my nose, followed by a tender kiss on each side of my face.

"Ellie," I warn.

"Where are we going?" she whispers across my mouth as she tries to coerce the answer from me.

"Mmm," I moan. Closing my eyes, I reluctantly back away. "If you keep doing that, there will be no surprise."

"Hmm." Ellie bites her bottom lip. "What's behind door number two?"

"How about you come with me right now and you can get door number one and bed number two." I extend my hand to hers.

"I guess." She shrugs her shoulders and walks right by me, not taking my hand.

My eyes betray me as they can't help watching every sway of her perfect ass walk toward the door. "Well?" She turns around like she is a supermodel on the runway. "We going?"

"Yeah."

Yeah? It's such a simple word, but when I'm around Ellie, sometimes even finding the simplest words seem like a difficult task.

"Then what are you waiting for?" She flings the door open, waiting for me to follow.

And I do. Because truth be told, I would follow her anywhere.

"Oh my God!" She spins around to face me after seeing the poster for her favorite cover band on the front doors of a local low-key bar. "How did you know?"

"As much as I want to take all the credit for this, I can't." I reach around her, pulling the door open. "Rain gave me a heads up."

"You are the best boyfriend ever!" Ellie jumps into my arms, peppering kisses all over my face.

"Boyfriend, huh?" I say, raising a brow.

"Lee, I think we are past the point of asking each other out. It's what you are, don't deny it." She slides out of my arms and heads inside, saying over her shoulder, "Plus, the things I want to do with you, I only do to boyfriends." She makes her way to the bar like she's been here a time or two.

By the time I make it up to the bar she is talking with some suit who looks like he could be a good ten years older than us.

"I'm Kevin. What's your name?" He holds out his hand—my cue to butt in.

Sliding my arm around her waist, I join in the conversation. "Well, Kevin, I'm going to do you a service and help you out here. Lines like that don't work." I give Ellie a little squeeze. "Let me show you how it's done."

Turning to Ellie, I move in closer. "I was blinded by your beauty. I'm going to need your name and number for insurance purposes."

"Yeah, right." Kevin waits for Ellie's reaction.

Placing a hand on my chest, she leans in to get a little closer, leaving our lips a breath apart. "Can you see me now?"

I nod.

"Good," she breathes. "My name is Ellie and if you give me *your* number, I'll give you something better," she purrs.

"Deal." I slam my mouth on hers.

Kevin clears his throat, but we continue putting on a show.

"Whatever, man."

Not forgetting he was the one who was trying to hit on my girl, I flip him the bird just as Ellie pulls away.

"So, Ellie, how about we get a table that is a little more private?" I grab our drinks, throwing down a twenty and waving off the change.

"Better luck next time, Kev."

"Fuck off."

"That was fun." Ellie spins around and walks backward.

"I tried to tell you, it's all in the pickup lines." I find a corner booth and set our drinks down, then grab her hand to give her a little twirl before she slides in.

"Why thank you, Mr. Scott." Ellie scoots across the seat. "Save me a dance?"

"I would love nothing more."

Ellie

This night has been perfect. Seeing Lee having fun and just letting loose was a sight yet to been seen, until now. With everything going on at home and the stress of work, Lee is never one-hundred percent relaxed. But tonight, he's a new man and I'm enjoying every second.

"How about that dance?" Lee stands up, offering his hand.

I take it, responding, "I would love to."

Pulling me straight into his arms, Lee walks us backward until we are in the middle of the dance floor. Hands on his chest, I can't help but explore.

"I love it when you touch me like that." Lee leans down and, mouth by my ear, he continues, "I've never—" He shakes his head once. "You. Your touch, it's intoxicating."

"Really?" I look up at him.

"Really." He gulps.

"You drunk yet?" I whisper as I snake my arms up and around his neck.

"You're something else, you know that?"

"Lee?"

"Yeah?"

"Kiss me."

He pulls back and his gaze falls to my mouth. His lips part as if he's going to say something, but the look in his eyes does the talking.

Slowly, he leans over and sweeps his lips against mine. Once, then twice, until I open for him. Lee has kissed me before—those kisses were consuming—but this one, it's different. Slow and tender, as if he's taking the time to memorize the taste of my lips.

He pulls away, his chest rising and falling. We both are at a loss for words, our kiss already saying so much.

Reaching up, with one hand still on my waist, he rests my head against his chest. I feel his heartbeat, beating in a rhythm that is just ours. We sway back and forth, lost in our own song until the next one starts.

Lee stills, tension suddenly flowing through his body.

"Lee?"

Dropping his hands, he takes a step back as if he is going to run. I've seen this look. I saw it the first night we met and then again when I thought he left for good. He fought it then and I need him to fight it now.

Lee doesn't want to run. I can feel it. He left the past at home, but right now, it's banging on the door.

"Lee, come back to me." I take a step closer. "It's just a song." Another step. "Nothing more." I repeat myself, trying to reassure him.

Reaching for his arms, I wrap them around me. Holding him, holding me. I begin to sway and sing. "Wise men say, only fools rush in." I reach up and cup his beautiful face in my tiny hands. "How can this song be so bad with words like that?" I brush my thumb over his bottom lip. I give him a kiss of reassurance and continue to sing as we move slowly to the song. "Some things are meant to be. Take my hand, take my whole life, too. Ohhh, for I can't help, falling in love with you."

Not saying a word, he holds me a little tighter and begins to lead us. Like two teenagers at a dance we repeat the motions over and over and over again. We dance, I sing. Until it's over.

Reaching down, he pulls my face to his. Breathing in a kiss like it's his last breath of air. "Thank you." He rests his forehead against mine and confesses his fears. "I was afraid of the song, what it meant, but the words, how you sang them—it's us."

"Lee." I try to look up. I need to see him. I need to touch him. I need his mouth back on mine.

"Don't." He holds a finger to my lips. "Some things are meant to be. Just like the song says and I know we both are dealing with a whole lot of fucked-up stuff, but Ellie, we came together for a reason. Call it fate or destiny or whatever, but I think it was meant to be. You have this way with me, of calming me."

"Lee." I raise my head.

"I love you, Ellie."

He loves me.

He loves me.

He loves me.

His words echo in my head. A smile slowly spreads across my face.

"Did you hear me, Ellie?" His lips curl.

He's back.

Lee's words weren't a desperate plea. They were a confession.

"I did." I nod.

"I love you," he repeats.

Hearing the words again, I can't hold back. "I love you too!" I shout as I leap into his arms, knowing he will catch me. I wrap my legs around his waist, throw my head back and laugh.

"That funny, huh?"

"Yeah." I nudge to the right, in the direction of everyone stopped. The band, the dance floor, hell, even the people at the bar are staring.

"Let them stare. Because I'm about to take the woman I love home." He begins to shuffle his way through the crowd, keeping me attached like I'm some kind of spider monkey.

And what can I say to that?

Chapter Twenty-Four

Lee

I'm standing in front of Ellie, the one person who believes in me and accepts me for the broken man I am, every jagged piece. I tried to push her away, but she pulled. And I fell. *Hard.*

The moments between leaving that dance floor to standing here, in front of each other, passed in a blur. We lost our clothes, one piece at a time, from the door to the bedroom. It wasn't a game or even a race. It was a need. A need to be skin to skin.

My heartbeat rings in my ears as I stand at the foot of her bed, thinking about those words. That song. The way her hand over my heart felt so right. How her body moved against mine. Although she stands before me stripped bare, I can't take my eyes off her face.

Staring into her eyes, I see desire there and I know she's remembering, too. The way she felt in my arms, the music, the lyrics. Something so simple, but meaningful. We stay like this for what feels like eternity, each of us waiting to see who goes first, afraid to break the moment.

I want to be the man to worship her, but before I make my move she leans into me, her lips finding mine. I deepen the kiss and try to take charge, but she steps back and places a gentle kiss on my chest before moving to the other side of my chest and then my bicep, before working her way around me in a slow circle. Her lips hover over my skin, back to shoulders, her hand trailing behind, brushing my heated flesh before completing a circle, coming to stand in front of me, lips over my heart. Almost like it's sealing in her affection.

I start to say her name, but only get as far as clearing my throat, before she takes my hand, and pulls me around to the side of the bed, asking me to lie down with just her touch. I climb onto the bed and tug her hand, pulling her with me. I'm propped up against pillows and she's draped across me, her hands exploring my naked skin, as if she's memorizing me. My hands fall to my sides, giving her complete control.

I know exactly how she feels. I did the same thing, committed every touch to memory. As her touch washes over me, the feel of what she's offering frees me from all thoughts. It chases away the past. I rest my head, but never take my eyes off of her.

She climbs on top of me and I can't help but reach out to steady her. My need for her grows as we lie skin to skin. My hands move down to her waist as she rocks against me.

My mouth captures her in a kiss that lets her know I'm hers. I give everything I have to her in that kiss, and everything I don't have. With it she also takes every bad memory, every broken promise, and replaces it with her own.

We pour it all out in silence, in the gentle exhales. A single tear slides down her cheek and if I wasn't lying down already, it would have brought me to my knees.

I shift us and gently roll, placing her beneath me. I rest on my forearms and cradle her face, wiping the tear with my thumb. I then capture her sadness and bring it to my mouth where I lick the pad of my thumb, never dropping my gaze. I make her a silent vow that I'll always kiss away her tears.

She smiles and my heart feels like it could burst. Sitting back on my knees I shift her legs and pull her to me. She reaches down between us, stroking me. Her hands on me are enough to nearly send me over the edge.

Pulling her hands in mine, I kiss her palms before lifting our joined hands above her head and I take my place between her legs. I pause one last time, just to make sure this is what she wants. She nods, even though her eyes say it all. I gently slide into her, exhaling as I go, amazed at how she feels made just for me. I struggle to take my time, enjoying the feeling of who we are when connected so intimately. I set the pace—slow, passionate and a promise of forever.

After some time, our mouths find each other. Our bodies make beautiful music together without making a sound. This moment is soulful and means something words could never capture. I feel her getting closer, her breath quickens before I feel her climax around me and I can't help but follow.

When we've both drained every bit we have to let go, I roll onto my back, taking her with me. I nestle my face into her neck, breathing her in, and she releases a contented sigh. As we fall asleep, our bodies still joined, I think to myself how some things are truly meant to be.

Ellie

Last night was incredible. Emotions flying, I wanted to feel his pain until his hope came back. I wanted to be that for Lee. Give him the light to his darkness with every kiss, every touch.

"Time to shower." Lee comes around to my side of the bed and picks me up, throwing me over his shoulder.

"Put me down." I kick and scream down the hall.

"Don't move or I'm going to drop you." He bends over to turn on the shower, letting it heat up before he climbs in and sets us both under the hot spray.

Being there in his arms I have never been so relaxed and felt completely taken care of by a man before. He grabs the soap and lathers up his hands before running them the length of my body. The journey is slow and tortuous as his hands move back up my legs, between my thighs, where I need him most. My desire grows but his touch isn't just sexual, it's like he's memorizing every curve.

It's empowering to see he's as turned on as I am. I can feel his desire brush against me as he stands, continuing his cleaning around my ribs. Soapy fingers work their way up my arms and massage my shoulders as he moves around behind me.

Pulling my hair to the side, he places a kiss on the back of my neck. My head falls forward against cool tile and his lips devour my neck as his fingers trail ever so slowly across my collarbone before moving lower.

"I was thinking," he whispers. My breasts rest in his palms and he twists my nipples ever so slightly.

"Uh-oh! That could be dangerous." I try to tease him but I'm having trouble thinking. He pinches my nipple.

"Funny." The fire he ignites causes me to back up against him, his hardness now pressed tightly against my lower back. "I was thinking, today we should go to the park."

"Okay," I moan. At this point I would do anything he asked of me. "Just don't stop."

He hisses and drops his hands, turning me to face him. "But first, I'm gonna take my time with you."

"Lee," I moan. "The par—"

"The park can wait, this can't."

The hunger in his eyes tells me he's not joking. And with that he drops to his knees in front of me and shifts my body so the spray hits me square on my sensitive chest. My back arches with the first swipe of his tongue, I reach out to steady myself.

"I got you," he murmers against my aching flesh, holding me in place. "I'll always catch you."

Chapter Twenty-Five
Ellie

I had a love-hate relationship with the park growing up. I loved it, but it came at a price—the park or music?—which I hated. But what kid didn't want to go there? It was a place where you could be anyone you wanted to be. Where you could run free and use your loudest outside voice. Play with kids you would probably never play with again. It didn't matter which side of the tracks you lived on. The park was just the park. No labels, no expectations. Free to be you. A kid.

I didn't catch on until I was much older and the park became less popular that it had been offered up as a distraction, anything to detour me away from my passion.

My parents would fight about my lessons. I wanted to play the drums, but instead ended up with piano lessons. Then when I showed interest in the guitar, they suggested the violin. At the time I thought I was winning, but it was actually my mom compromising with my father.

The park? It was another one of those compromises. When I showed interest in beauty pageants, my father agreed until he learned there was a talent competition. I was pulled, but where did we go? The park.

A field trip to a local theater where a popular musical was featured? We skipped it. My parents decided to surprise me with a fun-filled day at the park.

The park. As much as I love it, I resent it. Yet today, it feels good to be back. Being here wasn't a compromise or an obligation. It was a suggestion from the man I know would never make me choose.

Now here we are, bag across his chest, cooler in one hand and mine in the other, searching for a picnic spot.

"How about that tree?" He points at the one away from the playground, closer to the trails.

"It's perfect."

It really is. That old oak tree has been here since before I was born and it's one I know all too well. It's the exact same one my mother and I would set up a picnic under while we waited for my father to finish his run.

This tree was ours; we would lean against its thick trunk and sing about the day, making up songs about whatever was happening around us, a rare moment where it was just me and her enjoying what we both love to do.

Looking at the same spot as Lee spreads our blanket out I realize this was probably just as much my mom's secret as mine. I always thought my father had something against me and my music, but it was her, too.

I only heard my mother singing when she was in the shower or in the car. Sometimes at night when my father was working late or times in the park when it was just us. But never when he was around.

"Hey." Lee catches my attention. "You all right?"

Am I all right?

"I am. I mean, look at this." I smile as I take in everything Lee has brought. A thick cotton blanket he pulled from the back of his truck. A couple pillows to lay our heads on and the most beautiful spread of food. Cold cuts, a couple cold salads and a bottle of wine. "When did you have time?"

"Well, I cheated." He pats the empty spot beside him. "I called down to the restaurant and had them make this up. Took the cooler from my truck and packed it with ice."

"But when?"

"When you were getting ready." He chuckles. "You had the music blasting. It was the perfect time to call down."

"Good looking, intelligent and devious." I take the spot beside him. "I love it."

"I love you." I lean over for a quick kiss, one that is over way to soon.

"I love you too."

I will never tire of hearing him say those three little words. *I love you.*

We spend the day just lying here. Talking, cuddling, sometimes I read, while he sketches out a couple designs, and sometimes we just stare at each other. It's as if we are the only ones here. Just me, him and the open sky.

"You ready to go?" He begins to pack the cooler back up, setting it out of the way. The day of resting and snacking is winding down.

"I really don't want it to end," I confess. "I don't think I have ever felt this relaxed."

"Me neither."

"But I guess—"

"Hold on. I have an idea." He jumps up and jogs to the truck.

My guitar.

He takes his time walking back so he can be careful with it. The closer he gets the wider my smile becomes.

"I thought maybe you can play me something?" He sets it down in front of me while he takes a seat, resting against the trunk of my tree.

Our tree.

"Really?" I have the guitar out and in my hands before he can answer.

"Looks like I couldn't change my mind now even if I wanted to." He lets out one of those sexy laughs, the kind that vibrates through his whole body and mine. Causing my cheeks to heat.

I clear my throat. "Umm, no."

After playing a few songs, I find myself sitting in the middle of the blanket, legs crossed, guitar in my lap, and notebook spread out in front of me. The notes are flying, the words are scribbled. The inspiration is sitting against the spot that kept me company for years.

When I have it just right, I play through it one more time, humming the lyrics as Lee is busy sketching more designs.

"Bravo." He sets the pad down, leaning over to run his fingers through my hair before he claims my lips in a gentle kiss.

"Thank you." I turn my head, embarrassed by what I'm about to confess. I have never written a song for someone I cared about before. Life experiences, heartache, cheating, friendship...I've written about everything and anything, but a song about someone you love? Never. "It's for you. Hey! What's that?" I reach out and grab his notebook.

I can't believe what I'm seeing. I flip through the pages and see it's nothing but me playing my guitar.

"You weren't supposed to see that." He snatches the pad back from me.

"It's me," I whisper.

"Well, it's just your guitar and hands. I don't do faces." He smiles. "The eyes always look like they are oversized like those Japanese comic books. What are they called?"

"Mangas."

"Yeah, those." Lee makes a circle with each hand and holds them over his eyes. "They are huge."

"Well, this." I take it back to examine his work. "It's amazing. I love it."

"Well, well, well. I thought you would've been long gone by now." An unwelcome voice barges in on our time.

Lee jumps up, pulling me with him, and hides me behind him. "Who are you?"

"What? You mean Eloise Jane never told you about her parents?" My father's eyes narrow as he looks between the two of us.

I step in front of Lee, doing my best to take the hit. My father and I are at war and I refuse to let Lee be drawn in to it. Nathaniel Hawthorne is a powerful man and I will not let him manipulate his way into Lee's life.

"What do you want, Father?"

He looks behind him, pointing to the trails he used to run all the time. "Calm down, I didn't want anything. As far as I know it's a public park."

"It is," I retort, unable to come up with the words I really want to say. Sometimes when I'm around him I turn back into a defenseless child, always saying yes when inside I'm screaming no.

"Well, aren't you going to introduce us?" He takes a step forward, waiting for the introduction, but I don't give one.

"Lee Scott, sir." Lee steps forward, extending his hand. His grip firm, the shake controlled, but by who?

"Nathaniel Hawthorne, one of the top-rated security and corporate finance attorneys in the Midwest." He nods in my direction. "Also, Eloise's father."

"Nice to meet you, sir."

"You may call me Mr. Hawthorne." He drops Lee's hand and examines his own before he gives it a quick swipe against his running shorts.

Lee gives me an "is this guy for real" look. All I can do is wince and shake my head.

"What's wrong, Eloise? You've always been the talker. If I recall you had *so* much to say before you left for what I thought was Nashville."

That is just like him, never taking ownership of anything. It's always someone else's fault. He always used to say, "I may be wrong, but I will make them believe I'm right."

"I didn't leave, Father. You threw me out with nothing except a bag of clothes."

My father shakes his head and turns to Lee. "Can you believe this spoiled little brat?" He jerks his thumb toward me. "You show them a little tough love and they get all emotional about it." My father takes a step toward me, a smirk plastered across his face. "Honey, you are twenty-three years old. You wanted to live your own life? Well, I just gave you a little push."

"Holy shit! You are something else, you know that?" I take a step forward. Having Lee here gives me the extra strength I didn't know I had. "I tried to live my life. I tried to pursue a career, make my own choices, but they weren't *your* choices. Were they, *Father*?"

"Mr. Hawthorne, I would ask you to stay, but it seems as if you are upsetting my girlfriend. I need you to leave." Lee is now in front of me.

Not waiting for the outcome, I start packing up the rest of our things. If he isn't going to leave, then we will.

This trip to the park was just like the rest. Everything was always wonderful until *he* showed up.

"Lee Scott," my father says, not only grabbing Lee's attention, but mine. "Scott. Scott. Scott." He taps his chin, eyes narrowing. "Where have I heard that name before?"

Lee and I just look at each other, wondering what he is up to. We know my mother and his obviously had some kind of connection from our run-in with Sammy-Jo a couple weeks ago, but neither of us pressed her for answers.

"Have you been in trouble with the law?"

"No, sir," Lee quickly replies.

"Scott. Scott. Samantha Scott." My father's eyes widen. "You are Sammy-Jo's son."

There it is.

"Yes, Mr. Hawthorne, that is correct, but I was—"

"No need, son. Your mom was just like this one here." My father snorts. "It's all coming back to me now. Your grandparents had to raise you while she was off chasing her dreams." He turns to me. "See, your *boyfriend*," my dad seethes, "is a prime example of what happens when you try your hand in that industry. It's not made for having families." He glances back to Lee. "Isn't that right, son?"

"Mr. Hawthorne, Ellie is *nothing* like my mother," Lee spits back.

"You so sure about that?" My father inhales, then exhales. Being a lawyer, you have to choose your words carefully. This is him contemplating his next move. "Your mother and my wife were the best of friends. Anna wanted a family more than anything, more than music. That is why *my* daughter," he jabs his finger in my direction, "had two parents raising her. A mother and father. Your mom? She never wanted a family and especially not a child. Music City was and always will be her life."

"Father, what are you getting at?"

"My daughter here, she's a selfish one. Her mother and I tried to break her, but it didn't work. She always thought of herself, much like your mom, Lee."

"Your daughter is anything but selfish. She has never put herself before—"

My father cuts him off. "You didn't tell him, did you?" He pauses, looking between the two of us, waiting for me to answer a question, but I have no idea what he is asking. "She doesn't want children."

Lee turns toward me. I know he wants to ask me a million questions right now, but he also knows it will make things worse.

"Mr. Hawthorne, leave."

"So, as much as I would like to think she is worth saving. She's not." He locks eyes with me. "She. Is. A. Lost. Cause."

"Leave!" Lee shouts. "Now!"

Handing Lee my guitar, I grab the bag. "Lee, let's just go."

"No! We were having a pleasant day until he came up and invaded our spot. *He* can go." Lee takes a step closer to my father, his breathing rapid. "Go!"

"Son, if you want to get technical, we used to bring Eloise here when she was a child, therefore making it our spot."

Lee is fuming. If I were to throw water on him, I'm pretty sure it would turn right into steam.

"Lee." I tug on his back pocket. "Let's go."

Leaning down, he crashes his mouth onto mine, but it's more than a kiss. It's him proving my father wrong. It's him showing unity. It's him protecting me.

"Okay. Let's go," he whispers across my lips. "Home."

It's funny how life works. How you can grow up in a house with two parents, but it never feels like home.

Lee, he's my family now. *My home.*

Chapter Twenty-Six

Lee

It's been a crazy couple of days but today will be better, or at least according to Ellie it will be, because it's taco Tuesday.

"Tacos make everything better!"

Working side by side, Kyle and I tag team a stack of invoices accounting had issues with. Apparently, we were double-billed by the landscaper and not charged enough by electrical, which eventually would have come back to bite us in the ass.

Flipping through the next stack I come across an invoice from Hawthorne and Hawthorne, Attorneys at Law.

"What do you know about them?" I hold up the paper for Kyle to see.

"Well they are a pair of egotistical assholes, but they are the best at what they do." He takes the invoice and throws it to the side. "Why?"

"Well, I had a run-in with one of them at the park. It's Ellie's dad."

I use the term dad loosely. The way he used his words to attack isn't a man who respects his daughter. From what I know, Ellie has lived her life, for the most part, for him.

"Oh hell." Kyle exhales loudly. "What are you going to do?"

Great, even Kyle knows there could be trouble.

"She doesn't have a relationship with him. He more or less cut her off and kicked her out."

After our little outing, Ellie and I went back to my place where we just lay on the couch and chilled. Every now and then she would fill me in a little more on what took place with her parents. I didn't push. I know something about having to tell a difficult story. It takes time.

"That's a rough one, but I'll tell you this. It's my only advice I have for you." He spins around, his chair now facing mine. "As shitty as that situation was for her, that is still her mom and her dad. As dysfunctional as it seems, she *needs* them." He smacks me on the back and stands. "That's all I got. Good luck."

"That's it? That's your advice?" I lean over and bang my head against the desk. "He sucks. How can I encourage a relationship with him?"

"You don't. You encourage forgiveness. You don't have to ask for it to receive it." Kyle grabs his keys and slides his hard hat back on before opening the door. "You need to forgive to move on."

And just like that Kyle is gone, but his words linger.

I'm late and finding a place to park at Spotlight is becoming damn near impossible. Rebel Desire, a huge band, stopped in while passing through town on their US tour to play a short set for a local charity. All proceeds are going to Healing Hope, a shelter for domestic abuse victims.

After my third circle around the block, my phone begins to ring.

"Hello?"

"You still coming?" Ellie seems more excited than normal.

"Yeah. Just trying to find a place to park."

"I forgot! Cash Knight is here. I mean the band is, but hello!" She sighs dreamily.

I belt out a laugh. "Should I be worried?"

"Hell no. You are freaking Presley Aaron Scott." Her saying my full name doesn't seem so bad. If I were to be honest, I kind of like it. "Oh wait! Maybe you should come around back so you don't get mobbed. I want you all to myself," she purrs.

"Okay, now I know you are full of shit."

"Seriously, come around back."

"Heading that way now." I turn into the lot, trying not to hit all the fans chanting for Rebel Desire.

"I can't believe I never thought to tell you to park there. The spot belongs to me."

Thirty minutes, that is how long I have been driving around, but there is no need to tell her that. She would just feel bad and this is something neither of us could control.

"No worries. I know now—well shit!" I bang the steering wheel.

"What's wrong?" Her voice is laced with concern.

"Some Mercedes is parked in your spot," I say as I pull into the fire lane.

"Just tell them to move. They don't have a right to park there."

"I will. See you in a few minutes."

"I'll be here."

The phone automatically hangs up and I throw the vehicle into park and open my door, but when I do, the Mercedes door opens and Ellie's father steps out. He points to my passenger side.

Getting back in, I close my door and wait for him.

"It took you long enough to get here." Her father doesn't waste any time starting with the insults.

What the hell?

"I followed you from the lumber yard," he says, climbing in. "Number one sign. Serious boyfriends know where to park. She 'forgot,' didn't she?"

"You act like she has been living here for years. Plus, she doesn't have a vehicle. Out of sight out of mind," I give it back to him. There is no need for me to hold back now. Ellie isn't here.

"I'm going to cut the bullshit. Your relationship with my daughter can end in two ways."

"That's not happening," I cut in.

"Son, let me finish." He reaches over clasping a hand on my shoulder. "Hear me out."

"Five minutes or Ellie will come looking for me," I warn him.

"Two ways." Mr. Hawthorne holds up two fingers like this is some kind of school lesson. "First. She will either stay with you, live a happy life. I give it maybe two years, but then she will get the urge. Playing locally won't be enough. She will need more, but you can't give her that, can you? You will want kids, she will keep putting it off. Fighting will start and then eventually she will leave, accusing you of holding her back."

I can't help but nod at his words. I don't agree, but I'm taking it in, trying to respect the man enough to let him make his point before I face him with reality.

"Two. You play the supportive boyfriend. You make her believe she can do anything she sets her mind to and you will always be there to support her. So, she does just that. She takes on the world, they see her talent, they sign her, she records an album, then the tour. But wait, where does that put you?"

"We will make it work," I sputter.

"Will you? 'Cause if it's number one you fall under, you're screwed. Number two? Well, your grandmother puts a huge damper on that doesn't it?"

"You know nothing," I shout, my finger in his chest. This man isn't going to tell me about my life. It's mine.

He holds his hands up. "Hey, I'm trying to help you out. Save you from a life of shattered hopes and dreams." He laughs. "Okay maybe that *was* a little dramatic. We aren't in a courtroom."

"No, we are not."

"Listen, if it is the second scenario, you can't follow. Your life is here, with your Grans. Isn't that what you call her?"

"Not that I owe you an explanation, but I filled out an application for Lavender Springs Care Center and my mom is back. She's been helping—"

"Excuse me for interrupting." He holds up a hand to stop me. "But Sammy-Jo is the least reliable person there is. Like I said before, she and my daughter are cut from the same cloth. They get bored easily. They need *more*."

Her father hit me with a low blow. How can I argue with him when I've had those same thoughts?

"I realize this is hard for you, son, but I'm here to make it easier for you." He reaches into his inside suit pocket and pulls out a check book. "I know that Lavender Springs is pretty damn expensive. So, I'm going to cut you a check for a hundred thousand dollars to help pay for her expenses, in exchange for you to leave my daughter alone."

"No!"

"Fine, you're a smart kid from the wrong sides of the track. Greed suits you." He waggles his finger at me. "I like it." He voids the check. "How about a quarter of a million?" He begins to write it out, watching me out of the corner of his eye. "Yeah. You like that don't you?"

"I don't need your money." I narrow my eyes and try to fight back, but there is no winning with him.

"Sure you do." He rips out the check and waves it around for me to take it, but I don't.

"I do not. I have a job and I'm working on a project that will pay for a couple years of housing." I say the words with pride.

Because of my grandparents I learned the value of my worth. I have worked hard for everything I have. I got the job and I worked my ass off to prove myself. I did this!

"Then what?"

"What do you mean?" I crinkle my brow, confused to what he is getting at.

"Then what? You follow her to Nashville? What happens when the money runs out? You expect her to support you? Pay for your grandmother's living expenses?"

"Yes. I mean no! I don't know."

"Exactly. Just because she goes to Nashville, doesn't mean she will hit it big. She may not be able to support herself, let alone you and *your* baggage."

"I-I'm not leaving your daughter."

"Okay, obviously you need time for this to sink in." He rolls his eyes. "How about I leave this with you." He opens my glove box and places the check inside. "Just remember. The one condition is you let Ellie go."

And just like that, he's gone. In his car, backing out, and I'm left here with the weight of the world on my shoulders.

The money doesn't matter. What I have coming is enough to secure us a few years. Until we can figure out the rest *together*.

He may have given up on her, but I refuse to leave the one girl who stayed for me.

Chapter Twenty-Seven

Ellie

I can't believe it's finally happening. Everything I have wanted is going to be a reality.

My reality.

After reviewing my contract, I knew I had to renegotiate or decline the offer. The requirement to relocate to Nashville was not an option. I know, it was always supposed to be a part of my journey, but maybe now I want more. Maybe, just maybe, it was more about the escape than the dream. Here I have both.

I guess my mother's letter made me see exactly that. Did she have a passion for music? Yes. However, her love for her family was greater, and even though my father is the biggest douche known to mankind, she still loved him. She wasn't afraid of him. He didn't talk down to her or treat her like shit. He worshiped her. That, I could never fault my dad for. He was a great husband, just a shitty father.

But my mother's words stick with me. *"Your father loves you the best way he knows how."* Is this how he loves me? Why can't he love me a different way? One where he is proud and lets me explore my talents?

He's scared.

Her letter made so much sense and seeing him at the park just verified that. He's not the strong, in-control man I thought he was. No, he is one who hides behind his words, an armor to protect him from what he can't control.

I couldn't be controlled.

He thought he had the upper hand by showing me this "tough love" he talked about, but he underestimated me and the shock on his face proved just that. I guess I assumed since I was playing at Spotlight that word would get back to him. I was wrong.

I can't let my father get to me. Tonight is taco Tuesday! When there are tacos, the world is right. So, dammit, let today be good. Plus, I'm cooking, and I don't cook. Actually, I can't. I think tacos and spaghetti are the extent of my menu. Lee is the one who keeps our bellies full.

Glancing at my phone, I notice that Lee is late. He's never late so I give him a call and he quickly reminds me Rebel Desire is playing tonight. I love me some Cash Knight, but not at the cost of not being able to see my man. Give me my Lee.

I do feel bad that I forgot I had a parking spot. All this time Lee had to either walk a few blocks or pay for parking. Money he could have been saving.

A light rap on the door is a welcome distraction.

Lee.

Swinging the door open, I get ready to launch myself at him, but instead of walking in he says, "My name might not be Taco Bell, but I sure can spice up your night."

I just stand there.

"No?" he smiles. "How about this one." He clears his throat. "Hey girl, can you make my soft taco hard?" His lips are tight, trying to not laugh at his own line.

"Get your ass in here." I wave him in.

"How was your day?" Lee pulls me to him. Walking us backward, he kicks the door shut.

"It was good. I have some news," I tease him about the offer that is sitting on the coffee island.

"Mmm hmm." He begins to nuzzle my neck. "I missed you."

"I missed you, too."

"Shh, I'm talking to someone here. Oh, you missed my kisses? Well, let me fix that." He begins to nibble his way up to my ear before he whispers, "I love you."

"You're crazy." I push him away. "But I love you anyway."

I go over to stir the meat once before I begin to plate up our food. "So, did that guy give you a hard time?"

Lee freezes.

"What's wrong?"

"Nothing." He coughs. "How about a margarita?"

"Lee? Are you okay?" I set everything down and head over to the little bar set up in the kitchen. I wrap my arms around him from behind.

"Yeah. Of course. I just thought we should have some margaritas with the tacos," he replies, not even bothering to look at me.

"Okay." I drop my hands and back away. I can't force Lee to talk to me. Something happened and I'm not sure what it is, but if I keep pressing, I could make it worse. Especially if it has to do with his mom or Grans.

"I do have some news," I say again, hoping it will brighten the mood a little.

"Oh really?" He walks over to me, handing me a margarita before he takes a seat on the other side of the island.

"Yeah. It's a couple things really." I take a sip of my margarita, which is heavy on the tequila. "Wow! Trying to get me drunk?"

"Well, you know." He winks.

Okay, fun Lee is making a comeback. Good sign of a better night to come.

"Anywho, I talked to Rain today. Apparently, her parents decided that she needed an eco-friendly car so she is selling hers."

"That's great! Have tips been good?" He reaches across the bar, grabbing his plate and adding all the fixings.

"Yeah, really good. I should have enough to pay for it and still put some back for later."

"Uh-huh."

I catch Lee eyeing the contract sitting just a couple feet from him.

"And that's the second thing." I point to the papers.

"Just a second." He holds up one finger and stands as he pulls his phone from his pocket. He turns away before he answers.

"Hello?" He spins around, eyes wide. "How long?" He begins pacing. "Katie! How long has she been missing?"

"Lee, is everything okay?" I step in front of him, trying to get his attention, but my words fall upon deaf ears.

"Where is Mom? What? Call nine-one-one now!" he hollers into the phone before he ends the call.

Hands on his knees, breathing erratic, Lee begins to panic.

"Lee, look at me. Please."

He lifts his eyes.

"Good. Now breathe with me." I take a deep breath, pointing at my mouth. "Now exhale."

We repeat the motions until he stands up and says the words I was afraid I was going to hear.

"Grans is missing."

Lee

This is what I was afraid of. This is why I didn't want *her* helping. This is why I wanted a professional facility handling her care. So we could monitor her daily behavior, making preparing for the evenings easier.

I should have been there.

"Lee, she is going to be okay." Ellie, who decided I didn't need to be left alone, came with me.

"I hope so." I turn to look at her for a second, giving her a tight-lipped smile as I reach for her hand.

"Lee, your phone." She points to it as it lights up.

"Shit, Bluetooth isn't working. Answer it please."

Ellie slides the phone to life, presses the speaker and holds it up to me.

"Did you find her?"

"She's at a new construction site off of Tenth and Broadway," Katie cries into the phone. "She doesn't know where she is."

"What?"

"She's erratic, won't let anyone help her. She just keeps calling out for her husband," Katie sobs.

"I know where it is. Thanks, Katie." I nod toward the phone for Ellie to end the call.

"She's at the old drive-in."

The drive-in. It was everything to my grandparents. It was the place where they had their first date, first kiss and first everything else. I had to hear stories about how they steamed up a lot of windows in their day. I think Grans made my grandfather tell me those stories when he had the whole sex talk with me.

"The only drive-in I know about was torn down a few years ago and now a small shopping center is going in."

"That's the one. She's there roaming around, looking for my grandfather to tell her what's going on."

"We are almost there. Just..." She shakes her head. "I don't know what to say."

"Just be here. That's what I need from you. Be there to catch me when I fall. Because I will. This...it's what I've been afraid of." I give her hand a squeeze, drawing the strength from her to continue. "I've lost her, Ellie. She's gone."

"You don't know that. I've been doing a little research, and this comes and goes. Tomorrow could be a better day." She tries so hard to give me the hope I need to keep going, but even if this is true, what I'm feeling inside won't go away.

Dread.

Guilt.

Depression.

Anger.

I've zoned out, but the tires hitting the gravel lets me know we've made it.

"Where is she?" I sit up straight, straining my neck to see over all the emergency vehicles.

Ellie unbuckles her seatbelt. "Just park. Hurry, let's go." Her hand is on the handle, ready.

Just as I throw it in park, a fire truck takes off and clears my view. I see Grans fighting a couple paramedics who are trying to get her under control, probably to sedate her.

Slamming my fist down on the steering wheel, I throw my head back and scream "Fuck!" while I reach up and punch the roof once.

"Lee." Ellie places her hand on my shoulder. "She needs you. Go."

Nodding, I throw open the door and round the truck, reaching toward Ellie as she gets out. "I need you."

Hand in hand we run toward Grans. "Wait here," I tell Ellie.

Leaving her by the police car I run out to the scene, screaming to let Grans go.

"Jeanie!" I shout. "It's me, your Paulie." I use the nickname she often called my grandfather.

"Paul? Is that you?" She calms herself and searches for me. "Get off me. I told you he would be here. When he sees what you did to this place—"

"I'm here, Jeanie." I walk toward her and she finally sees me.

"No!" she screams before throwing herself to the ground.

"Grans!" I take off in a full sprint. "Grans! I got you." I carefully put a hand under her arm.

"Get off me! Get off me! Get off me!" Grans repeats, yanking away from me. Sobs continue to rack her body.

"Let me help you." I try to lift her up. "We need to get you to the hospital."

Grans looks down at herself and lets out a huge, shrill, blood-curdling a scream. "What did you do to me? Where is Paulie?" She searches the area frantically. "Paulie? Paulie?"

"I don't know what to do!" I turn to the paramedic, pleading for him to help.

"She's going to hurt herself if we don't sedate her." He reaches into the back of the truck and grabs what he needs. "But the closer we get, the more irate she becomes."

"I'll hold her."

"I can have one of the officers help." He offers me a way out, but I can't take it. I need to do this. Seeing her being restrained is heartbreaking. If anyone is going to hold her down it will be me so I know I'm not hurting her.

"Lee, what can I do?" Ellie is behind me.

"Go. Just leave." I reach into my pocket to throw her my keys but they must have fallen out when I was running toward Grans.

"I'm staying." She reaches for my hand, but I can't help but jerk away. If I feel her touch I'll break, and right now, I can't. I have to stay strong.

"No!"

"Lee?"

"Go!" I yell a little too loudly. "Spare keys are in the glovebox. I'll take her car. Just go."

"I can stay." She fights, thinking she knows what I need and maybe she does, but if I let her comfort me, I can't be strong enough for Grans.

"Go, Ellie! Now!"

"I love you." She begins to silently cry as she turns to leave.

I did that to her. The promise of always kissing away her tears—*broken.*

Chapter Twenty-Eight
Ellie

I wanted to be his strength, be what he was for me time and time again—especially with my father—but I couldn't. He told me to leave and I did. I did what he wanted. But not what he needed. I should have stayed.

Maybe my father was right. *Selfish.* A selfless person would have fought to stay.

Climbing into the driver's side, I reach into the glove box and search for the key.

What in the world?

"No! No-no-no-no-no!" I hold a check made out to Lee from my father. "Please God, no!" I drop the paper like it's on fire, the burn blistering my soul.

Two hundred and fifty thousand dollars. Is that what I'm worth? A quarter of a million dollars? And for what? For him to take care of me? To leave me? To jeopardize my career?

Is this why he was acting funny? I thought something was bothering him, maybe something about his grandmother, but was it guilt?

Glancing up, I see Lee standing there where I left him. I watch him watching his Grans as they work on sedating her. My heart hurts for a man I thought I knew. I glance between him and the check. Maybe I didn't know him at all. Seeing the broken look on his face I can almost understand. Almost. Putting the key in the ignition, I start the truck and back away. It's what he wanted. It's what I'm going to do.

Leave.

Tears blur my vision as I throw stuff into my bag. I want to stay.

Stay!

For him. For us. But he just gave me two hundred and fifty thousand reasons to walk away.

I should have known my dad wouldn't stay out of my life. I'm angry at him. I'm angry at Lee for making me think he was different and I'm angry at myself for being prepared to throw it all away.

One bag. It's what my life has been reduced to. Twenty-three years of life and it all fits into one bag. Clothes. I'm nothing but what I wear.

Life experiences. I wasn't allowed them and when I tried to have some, I was brought back to the start. A *"do-over"* as my father called it.

Now I'm free to make my own decisions. Free to become the woman I have been searching to be. Being with Lee, receiving that contract? It was my start, my new beginning. But somehow, I wasn't doing that right either, because my father and two hundred and fifty thousand dollars created a *do-over.*

Now I'm standing in front of the mirror, bag in hand, ready to leave and never look back. Reaching out, I touch my reflection, looking into my own eyes. Empty and hollow. The smile that was there is gone.

"I hate yoooooooooou!" I scream at the person I am. "You are nothing but a coward." I smack the mirror. "You didn't fight," I repeat over and over again.

I want to kick. I want to scream. I want to cry for the girl I was and the woman I wasn't allowed to become. He did this to me. He stole away everything I was meant to be.

"I didn't fight." I fall to the floor, face in hands and I do exactly that. I cry.

I'm not sure how much time passes, but as the final tear runs down my cheek, I realize my sky has been crashing down for a while now and it's up to me to either fall with it or fly.

I want to soar.

Wiping the tear with the pad of my own thumb, I make a promise of never letting anyone else catch my tears again. A promise I'm willing to make sacrifices for in order to keep.

I was set to leave. I was going to Rain's to switch out vehicles, but I didn't. I kept going and headed to the one place I should have gone a long time ago.

I may have had my share of arguments with my father, but I never fought for myself. I never fought for who *I am*.

I pull into the drive, and after parking the truck, reach into the glove box and pull out the check. The tiny piece of paper that managed to take everything that was good in my life and make it into an illusion.

Gone. Just like that.

Running up to the house, I don't bother to knock. I barge in just like he did into my life. Unannounced. A surprise attack.

"Get down here you son of a bitch," I scream, standing in the middle of the foyer, waving the check around. "What? You afraid to come down and face me? Is it easier to hide from this?"

"Eloise." My father comes up behind me, a tumbler of scotch in hand. "I wasn't sure if I would see you again." He comes to stand in front of me, his step never faltering. My father, always confident.

"Why is that, Father? Didn't you think once you paid him off that I would come running back home?" I throw the check at his feet. "Quarter of a mil? Is that all I'm worth to you?" I laugh. "Nice to know what you think of me."

"Eloise, why do you have to be so dramatic? Of course you are worth more." He places his hand on my arm.

"Don't touch me." I jerk away.

"I actually shelled out double that to ensure you *would* come home." He brings the tumbler up to his chin, finger out, and presses it against his lips, calculating his next words before he takes a pull of the dark liquid.

"What?"

There is no way he gave Lee two checks and Lee actually cashed one, is there? I can't. I just can't.

"I just didn't give your boyfriend enough credit. I thought I had him there, but he fought. Fought so damn hard." He lets out an evil laugh and drains his glass. "Apparently, he has 'plans.'" He makes quotation marks with his fingers, shaking his head in amusement. "If he wasn't so damn supportive of your hobby, I might have actually liked him." He walks over to the decanter a few feet away and pours himself another drink.

"It's not a hobby." I'm at a loss for words, trying to figure out what he meant by *double*.

"Do you think you can make a living at this? Do you?" He walks over to the check, picks it up and stuffs it in his shirt pocket. "Let's play out a scenario. Let's say you stay with this boy, then what? You leave for Nashville together? You expect him to leave his life and his grandmother to come follow you around?" He presses his lips together. "And if he does, are you going to support him? His job requires him to work on location and this *'plan'* of his will eventually run out of money. Then what? His grandmother needs the care."

"It doesn't have to be that way," I counter. I hate that I'm even having this discussion with him. I came here to rip up that check and never see him again.

"And that," he points his finger at me, "is why you are selfish."

Am I?

"How can that be selfish, to want the person you love to be with you?" I take a step forward, then another. "Isn't that what you did with Mom? You wanted her with you so bad you gave her an ultimatum? Me or the music?" Another step. "That's right. I know all about it. She came back to you because she loves you." I'm close enough I jab him in the chest. "And because she loves me, but don't think she has no regret, because she does."

"What is going on in here?" My mother comes around the corner.

"Eloise here thinks she knows it all. Nothing to concern yourself with, Anna."

My mother, who would normally back my dad up, surprises us both by coming to stand by me. *With* me. A silent show of support.

"Ellie Jane, what's going on?"

"Thank you," I mouth, meaning much more than just those two words. Thank you for the note. Thank you for the words of encouragement. Thank you for the show of support. Even if it's late, it's better than never. "Dad paid off my boyfriend, but I'm still trying to figure out why. Paying him off would have sent me on my way to the one place he never wanted me to end up: Nashville."

"Nate? Is this true?" she demands.

"I had to do it." His eyes move from mine to hers, pleading. "It was a gamble."

"I can't believe you. You are a pathetic excuse for a parent." I start toward the door. "So, now what? Lee has the money—"

"He won't cash it," my father interrupts.

"But you said you paid double that."

"To Sammy-Jo. She cashed a check," he confesses, and my mother gasps.

"You did what?"

I can't believe what I'm hearing. He gave an addict more money than she has probably ever made in her whole life and sent her on her way.

"I paid his mother to leave," he says without an ounce of remorse.

"But why? What would that do for you? How would that keep me from leaving?" I look at my mom. "Why would he do that?"

"I don't know honey. Nate?"

"I saw you. I watched you in the park." He tilts his head from side to side in irritation. "He loves you. He *supports* you. I knew with him in the picture you would have made all your dreams a reality."

"It still doesn't make sense," I insist. "Nothing about this does."

"I'll make this simple for you. You need your boyfriend. Your boyfriend needs his grandmother. His grandmother needs care. I needed him gone. So, I gave him the resources he needed to choose. Either you or his grandmother."

"He chose his grandmother," I say under my breath.

"No, he *didn't* choose." My father rolls his eyes. "Which didn't surprise me."

"I'm not following," my mother says.

"I underestimated his feelings. So I decided to play with his, to save you." He reaches up and rubs his day-old scruff, the confession obviously hard for him. "I knew Sammy-Jo was the weaker of the two and I knew your boyfriend had deep-seated mommy issues." He looks away as he comes clean. "I paid his mom to leave. If she left he would see that you all were the same, that you would eventually leave him too. Seeing it would cause him to spiral downward and send you away."

"What gives you the right to play God?" My mother steps

forward. "You didn't have the right to play it all those years ago and you don't have the right now." She turns away from him and stands by me, taking my hand in hers. "I won't let you."

"But every scenario you counted for still put me in Nashville following my dreams. I don't get it. You dedicated your whole life to making sure that wouldn't happen."

I don't know how to feel, too many emotions are coming forward. *Anger. Sadness. Regret.* I missed out on so many opportunities growing up because of this.

"Eloise Jane, all your life you just wanted someone to support you, to believe in you. I knew if I took that away, you would fail and come home." My father's eyes bulge at his own admission.

"Nate!" my mother shouts.

Tears stream down my face. The man who is supposed to push me toward my dreams and show me that I can do anything fought my whole life to make sure that never happened.

"You're wrong." I walk over to him. I take the check out of his pocket, rip it up and throw it on the floor. "I believe in myself and that is all the support I need."

I stand there, looking at the man who has hurt me. Who knocked me down. Who told me I would be nothing.

I am something.

Leaving, I set out to sing *my* song the way it was meant to be heard, escaping the gravity that pulled me down. From here on out, I will soar into the light, leaving the darkness behind. I will be *weightless*.

Chapter Twenty-Nine

Lee

I tried to hold on to the only mother I have ever known. The one who raised me to be the man I am, who refused to give up on me, who told me I could be anything I wanted to be.

She's gone. And I feel like a failure. I let her slip through my fingers.

My hands shake, I struggle to breathe. I'm nothing without her. I gave up on her. I can't do this *without her*.

I thought I was doing the right thing by sending her there, but did I? If this is how it's going to be, how can it be a life worth living? There has to be something more.

More.

More.

More.

Is there more? Is this it? Oh God, please don't let this be it.

I need her to be the Grans I remember her to be. Just one more day. One more second to tell her I love her.

There are promises of tomorrow, of a good day, but what if there isn't? What if today was her tomorrow?

I need Ellie. I need her to tell me it's going to be okay. I need her to hold me and make me feel the way only she can. I need her to tell me I can get through this. I need her to give me more.

More.

More.

More.

There is more than this. Ellie has shown me that she makes everything better just by being her. And I pushed her away.

It's late. I should have called. I should have explained. I should have done everything different, but I didn't.

I told her to go. I sent her away when she tried to be there. Now, I'm sitting in front of her door, hoping it's not too late. Hoping she stayed.

"Lee?" Ellie whispers.

My eyes drift up to see my beautiful dreamer standing there with a bag in tow, and I lose it.

Sobs rack my body as I let it pour out. I cry for the woman who raised me and the woman I wanted to spend my life with. Both gone. I've lost them both.

"Oh Lee." I hear the bag fall and Ellie is right in front of me, on her knees. She pulls me into her lap and I let her. I'm a weak bastard who is willing to take everything she has left.

"They diagnosed her as stage five with a rapid decline. I've lost her, Ellie. I've lost her."

"Oh God." She brushes hair out of my face. "I'm so sorry, Lee. So, so sorry," she repeats over and over again.

"And I lost you." I look up into her eyes, which mirror mine—bloodshot and teary.

"Lee." She shakes her head.

"Just tell me it's not too late." I stand up, taking her with me. "Tell me that isn't what I think it is." I nod to the suitcase behind us.

"We need to talk." Tears stream down her face. I reach to wipe them away, but she catches my hand, letting them fall.

"Ellie." I shake my head, not wanting to accept what just happened.

Broken promises.

"Let's go inside." She walks past me and unlocks the door I fixed. The memory of our first kiss replays in my head as she continues. "I think we need to start from the beginning."

Following her in I turn, pushing her up against the wall, in a desperate move to make her remember.

"Are you a time traveler? Because I can see you in my future." I choke back the tears and force a smile.

"Don't." Ellie gives me a look, her lips tight. She is fighting back more than I realized. She can see right through me. She knows why I'm here. "We really need to talk."

She steps away from me. "Lee, please come sit down with me." She extends her hand in an offering.

I accept. I try to take control and move us to the bed. "No." She shakes her head and pulls us toward the couch. "Over here."

"Okay."

We sit down beside each other. She continues to hold my hand, bringing it to her lap where she rubs circles with her thumb, comforting me.

This is it.

"I know about the check," she blurts out.

"Ellie, It's not what you think." I turn to look at her. "I promise. I didn't cash it. I wouldn't. Your father—"

"I know, Lee." She gives me a weak smile.

"Ellie, you have to know you are more to me than just a piece of paper. You are worth so much more."

"Thank you." She continues to rub circles. "That's not all. Your mom. She left because of my father." Ellie looks at me out of the corner of her eye.

"What?" I stand up, yanking my hand out of hers.

"My father, he paid your mother to leave. The same amount he offered you."

"Why would he do that? What does my mom have to do with us?"

"I'm so sorry, Lee." She gulps. "Because of me. He wanted you out of my life and he thought he could either pay you to leave or he would pay your mom and you would react to her skipping out again, thinking I was just like her."

"That's fucked-up on so many levels. Fucked-up that he even thought of something like that." I begin to pace the floor. "Fucked-up that he would do that to hurt you. Fucked-up that it worked."

"It only works if we let it." She stands in front of me, reaching for my hands.

"I saw the contract."

She takes in a deep breath and exhales. "I was planning to tell you about that, but then we got the call—"

"You're leaving me, too," I interrupt.

"Yes." She nods. "But no. I'm here Lee, with you." She brings my hand up and places a kiss on my knuckles. Everything I should be doing to her, but I'm the selfish bastard. I'm the one who is taking everything I can get to just make it through the day.

"It's not forever. It's just a few weeks."

"Were you going to tell me?" I nod at the bag over by the front door.

She looks over her shoulder to see what I am suggesting. "No. I wasn't, but I was angry. I thought you took the money, Lee."

"I would never." Her thinking I would do that stings.

"I know, but a part of me almost understood why."

"Ellie?" I laugh in disbelief.

"Once I found out, I knew I had to see you. I knew we needed to talk."

"Ellie? What are you saying?" I drop her hands and move to the bed to get some distance.

"I'm saying that I love you Presley Aaron Scott." She comes to stand in front of me, her beautiful hazel eyes capturing my heart. "I'm saying that I never even thought about staying, until you. You are my family. You are my heart. You are my *home*."

She stretches her neck, asking for me to kiss her. So I do. I take her mouth. I own it. I claim this moment and every memory before. This kiss is accepting what I have done. I made her stay when she needs to go.

Breaking our kiss, breathing erratic, I try to form the words I never wanted to say. "You. Need. To. Go."

Looking around she laughs. "It's my place, silly."

"No. You need to go to Nashville." I pull her over to sit next to me. "I did this to you. I made you want to stay when you have always wanted to go."

"That's not true." She begins to get irritated.

"Yes, it is. You were headed out before your father took everything. It was your dream. Me? Having a family? It's not what you want."

"How do you even know what I want?" She jumps up, obviously angry.

"We want different things. Nashville, I can't make it part of my dream. Not right now, and how is that fair to you?"

"You don't have to make it your dream. You just have to support mine," she fires back.

"Listen to me." I stand face-to-face with the woman I love. The woman I'm setting *free*. "My love can't heal your scars when they can't even heal my own. My love can't rescue you. Only you can, by seeing your dreams through. No regrets."

She leans forward, her lips brushing mine, tears soaking her face. "You will never be a regret."

I look at Ellie, accepting her words. *You will never be a regret.* I wanted for this to be a tender moment, for her words to heal me. So I'll use my touch to do the same for her. To give her something to remember me by and hopefully bring her home to me.

Home.

Thinking about everything she is to me makes my heart dance and I no longer can contain myself. This isn't going to be slow and soft. We don't have time for that. Every moment I have left with Ellie, before she leaves, is precious and I'm going to make use of every. Last. Second.

I reach for Ellie and she wraps her arms around my neck. I find the spot on her, *my spot*. Her pulse, jumping erratically, matches my heartbeat. I grab her waist, pulling her up, and she wraps her legs around mine.

We become a desperate tangle of limbs and mouths, saying everything with touch we don't have a chance to say with our lips. It's like coming home and saying goodbye all at once.

I lay her on the bed and we take turns stripping each other bare. A beat passes as we drink each other in, one last look of her perfect body, to keep me warm on lonely nights. Until she comes back to me.

She has to.

I shake away the dark thoughts and focus on the fact that she's here now. Grabbing a condom, I climb between her legs and the moment our lips connect we're back to a frenzied pace, relishing each other's embrace. Every touch accepting what we can't control. Every touch trying to heal but accepting it can't.

As I slide into her, she moans into my mouth and hearing her calling my name in the throes of passion is the sweetest sound I've ever heard.

My lips hover over hers, drinking her in. Her passion, her ecstasy, her song.

Our song.

"Ellie?" I turn my head to look at the woman who saved me from myself. The woman who breathed life back into my soul.

"I know," she admits. The unspoken words were all that need to be said.

"I don't want you to go," I confess. "I'm scared to face this alone."

"No," she whispers, reaching down and grabbing my hand. "You're never alone, Lee." She takes our joined hands and places them over her heart. "You're here. *Always.*"

Leaning in, I gently claim Ellie's warm lips with a kiss that is shaky and unsure. A goodbye.

"Now what? Where do we go from here?" She turns her head so we are looking eye to eye, and a lone tear slowly falls down her cheek. Bringing my hand up, I capture it with my thumb and put it in my mouth, taking everything I can before she's gone.

"You go." I curse the words I don't want to say, silently begging for her to not listen.

Don't go.

"I go."

Please don't.

"We heal."

We will.

"We will."

Together.

"I love you."

Forever.

"I love you too."

Stay.

"So much for taco Tuesdays." Ellie kicks the rocks around in the parking spot she forgot she had.

"Yeah. They kinda suck," I agree. "What time did Rain say she will be here?" I look at my watch for the millionth time, willing it to stop. To give me more time. Just one more day.

"Any minute." She turns her head to the side, sucking her lips in.

"Ellie, don't cry." I bring my hand up to her face and get her to look at me.

"I'm not." She laughs as I wipe the tears away. Not one falling.

"You're a bad liar."

"Stop." She smacks my chest. "Lee?"

"Yeah?"

"Ask me to stay. 'Cause I will. I'll do it for you." She says it. The words I have craved to hear.

"I can't do that." I pull her face to mine. "Not because I don't want you to, but because you deserve more. I can't give you more until I can move on. I have to forgive and forgiving is a work in progress."

"You are a good man, Presley Aaron Scott."

"Ahhh." I pull her in, my mouth instantly going to my spot. "Go. Show Nashville what I already know."

Her hands fly up and rub my back, silently reassuring me that I'll be okay. And I will. She's shown me that.

Pulling away, I see Rain parked across the street. "Your ride's here."

"Don't look. I can't leave if I don't know." She begins to frown.

"Don't do that." I touch her lips, anything to feel her one last time. "You smile. You show the world that contagious smile of yours."

"Ellie!" Rain shouts. "We have to go or you will miss your flight."

Grabbing Ellie's hand, I walk her to the car and open the door for her to slide in.

"I guess this is goodbye." I pull her to me and wrap my arms around her one last time.

"Don't." She puts her hand between us, holding a finger up to give her a minute to say what she needs to say, fighting back the tears. "You don't get to say that. You don't get to say goodbye."

"Ellie, you need to get going." I help her in the car, but just as I'm about to close the door she jumps back out.

"See you later. Because I will. I'm coming back for you, Lee Scott." She smacks me with a kiss before hopping in and closing the door. She waves at me as Rain pulls off.

Promise me, Ellie. Promise me you will come back.

Chapter Thirty

Lee

"Excuse me?" I say, staring across the desk in confusion at Sandy, the co-owner of Lavender Springs. "How is that even possible?"

I had a meeting scheduled for today to finish the paperwork and pay the deposit for Grans since moving day is tomorrow, but instead of taking my money they are telling me it's been paid for.

Impossible.

"The next year, it's paid in full." She clicks on the mouse, running through Grans' account. "Ah! Yes, you see, right here." She turns the screen to me. "It was paid by a Samantha Scott two weeks ago."

"That can't be right." I shake my head. "She left town two weeks ago."

"It's possible for a mistake to be made, but Mr. Scott, we are not going to make…" A few more clicks. "As I was saying, the money was dropped in our account the same day as it was credited." She pulls open a drawer and digs through her files. "Here it is." She passes me an envelope.

"What's this?"

"There was a comment here that I'm to give this to the person who comes in to pay for your grandmother's suite." She stands, and I follow. "Please, take your time. I know this can be a difficult adjustment. I'll give you a moment." Sandy reaches out, shaking my hand in both of hers. "We look forward to having Jean stay with us. See you tomorrow."

"Thank you." I nod as she walks out, shutting the door behind her.

The envelope is from my mother. The penmanship is unforgettable as it's the only thing I had from her for years. A store-bought birthday card with a simple *To Presley, From Mom* on the inside. No words of wisdom or well wishes, just a card that I'm sure my Grans forced her to sign on one of her visits.

Sliding my finger under the flap, I open the envelope to pull out a handwritten letter.

Presley,

I know you don't like your name, but to me, you are Presley Aaron Scott and you will forever be mine.

I have failed you so much as a mother and I have apologized time and time again, but the past few weeks I have spent with your grandmother and seeing the way you are with her, I'm not going to apologize anymore. I know I made the right decision.

Lee, as much as you want to think things would have been better if I had been home, they wouldn't have. You, my son, are amazing and I'm so proud of the man you have become, but that was because of your Grans. She loved you as if you were her own. She is your mom, Lee. No matter how desperately I want to be, she holds the title.

Your grandmother brought me back to you. She called me upset. She knew, Lee. She knew she was slipping under and she didn't want you to bear the burden. All she wanted was for you to be happy and have a family of your own. To experience the joy you gave her. And if I could help, I wanted to.

Ellie is a sweet girl and looks so much like her momma. Anna, her mother, was my best friend and had so much talent. I was often jealous of how it came so naturally to her, but in the end we both had to choose. I was the selfish one. I'm sorry.

But if I could do one thing, if I could make things easier on you now, I would and that is why I did what I did. Nate Hawthorne came to me with an offer I couldn't refuse. The agreement was that I leave town.

Just know, I didn't spend the money. As soon as I cashed the check, I paid for a year for your grandmother. The rest is in your grandmother's savings account. I've added you to the account. They just need your signature and are expecting you.

I hope you can forgive me, but Lee, I needed to do this not only for you, but for me, too. I have taken so much from your grandparents with nothing in return. I just wanted to do something this time. This is all I had. It's all I could give.

Please forgive me.

I love you! xoxo

Mom

They say time heals all wounds. I'm not sure I believe that to be a hundred percent true, but it has helped. And this letter, it's the start to forgiveness and moving on.

"Knock knock." I rap on the door to Grans' hospital room. The nurse already gave me a heads-up that she was having a good day, which is just what I need. Especially after the letter I received.

I just need her. I just need to hear her voice and know that it's my Grans.

"Hello."

"Tomorrow is moving day. How are you feeling about it?" I set the flowers I got her by the windowsill and pull up a chair.

"I want to go home." Grans' bottom lip begins to quiver.

"I know." I take her hand in mine. "But Grans—"

"It's what's best. I know. The nurse was telling me all about it today." She turns her head to look the other direction before she comes back to me.

Even though this is a good day, the spark that Grans used to have in her eyes is gone, but today she knows my name, she recognizes me. And for that, I'm grateful.

"They have bingo." I try to perk her up. When I was younger, Grans would drag me along to Friday night bingo. *"Presley, you're my lucky charm. Better than any fluffy-haired troll,"* she would say as she ruffled my hair.

This bingo is to stimulate certain sections of her brain, but it's still an activity that residents loved.

"Grans, I need to talk to you about something." I reach out and carefully grab her hand. She squeezes it, squeezing my heart.

"What's on your mind, my sweet boy?" I close my eyes at the sentiment.

"The house?"

"Oh yes! How is it holding up? Did you grandfather put a fresh coat of paint on the porch?" she asks, her good day slowly fading.

"Not yet, but I can do that for you." I smile.

"That's my boy. Always so helpful." Grans raises her hand to ruffle my hair. "You make your Grans proud. You know that?"

Choking back the tears, I reply, "I try."

"You are going to make a fine husband someday. Just like your grandfather."

"I hope so, Grans." I turn and swipe the tears away.

I was hoping I could talk to her about selling the house, give myself the peace of mind to do so, but I can't. If I were to be honest, I'm not sure if I'm ready to give it up anyway.

"So, about the house, is there anything you want me to bring tomorrow?"

"Biscuit. I sure do miss him."

"Grans, Biscuit is…" I search for words that won't upset her.

"Presley, the pillow." She rolls her eyes. "Geesh."

"I'm sorry." I'm at a loss for words. Sometimes I'm not sure how to handle these situations, afraid I will be the one to trigger her.

"Scoot closer, Presley." She waves her hand at me. "Tell your Grans everything your grandfather has been doing since I've been locked up."

"Well…" I place my arms on the bed, settling in for a couple hours of stories or until the nurse kicks me out. I'm not quite sure how old she thinks I am, but I dig deep and recall a few funny ones that I'm sure will make her smile.

Making me smile.

It's been a month since I last saw Ellie. We've only been able to talk a couple times due to our conflicting schedules. With work and the flipping project, and her recording through the day and playing at night, sometimes texting is our only option and it's been about a week since we have said more than the typical *"Hey!"* or *"I can't wait to see you."*

Me: I've been counting down the days.

Normally it takes her hours to respond to one text. I usually get a response before her nightly gig, but right now, I see the three dots of hope: A pending message.

Ellie: They pushed my schedule back. :(

Me: That sucks. Any certain reason?

Ellie: Can't rush perfection.

Ellie: How's Grans?

I want to tell her all about it. Tell her how Grans had a great day, but I need more than questions from her. I need to find out when she's coming home.

Me: She's hanging in there.

Ellie: Have you talked to your mom?

I have a feeling she already knows the answer to this. Last week I ran into mom while visiting Grans, and instead of brushing her off or giving her the cold shoulder, we actually had a nice conversation. I found out that she works in a bar that Ellie plays in.

Leave it to Ellie to help from hundreds of miles away.

Me: Yeah, just last week.

Ellie: That's good. ;)

Me: Actually, it really was. Thank you.

Ellie: I have no idea what you're talking about ;) xoxo

Me: Have you talked to your parents?

After finding out my mom took the bribe money from Ellie's dad, I instantly went and withdrew it and returned it, minus the cash Mom used for the payment.

The shocker? Mrs. Hawthorne apologized for all the trouble they put me through. I told her it wasn't me who they needed to apologize to.

Ellie: My mother flew out this past weekend.

Ellie: Lee, it was nice.

Me: That's great news.

Ellie: She even got up on stage and we did a duet. She killed it.

Me: Can't wait to see it. You two taking the stage when you come back?

I drop a hint, hoping she will give me a little something. Anything.

Ellie: Maybe ;)

Ellie: Oh hey! They are hollering for me. TTYL.

I start to type that I miss her or "see you soon," knowing she won't see it until later, but then the dots pop back up.

Ellie: I miss you so much, Lee. xoxo

Lee: Same here!

Ellie: xoxo

Sliding the phone back into my pocket, I try not to let it get me down and ruin the day I'm having. Each day she's gone seems longer and longer. I feel my hope starting to slip. But then I have days like today when I see Grans and I know I did the right thing. For both women in my life.

Grans may not realize it but I'm still learning from her. She showed me what being selfless really is, and letting Ellie go was me doing that. Putting someone I love first. Just like my Grans did all those years.

I keep holding on and waiting for the day she comes home. *To stay.*

Epilogue

Lee

Two Weeks Later

I walk into Spotlight after searching for a parking space for what seems like forever, before saying screw it and parking in Ellie's old spot. A spot that fortunately remains vacant. Of all the places to grab a beer it had to be a place that reminds me of the girl I love, the one girl who wanted to stay. The girl I encouraged to leave.

It was for the best. It's what she needed to do. Prove to herself what I already know, what everyone knows — that she can make it.

And I needed to deal with my Grans, and even my mom. I needed this time to live for me. Make something of myself, so I could be the man she needs. Someone not living in the past.

Kyle waves me over, and I shake off the pity party. "Hey man, you made it."

"Yeah. Turns out I didn't have plans after all." I try to hide the disappointment in my voice. Ellie didn't make it home this weekend, she has some big gig she's excited about. I'm happy for her, but damn I'm dying to see her.

Hold her.

She said she would only be gone a month, but now it's been six weeks.

I thought about driving down to surprise her, but with work, this flip project and now my furniture business taking off, I just couldn't swing it. Thanks to Ellie and her recommending my guitar stands, I'm getting all kinds of calls about custom pieces.

I feel a little guilty that I've been zoning out. She's invading my thoughts like she always does. So I focus and catch up with Kyle. We go over the coming week's projects and discuss the possible early sale of the current flip. An out-of-state corporation wants to come in and buy it as-is. Drew and Kyle want to sell, but they said I have the final decision since I was counting on the full profit.

I'm all in. It's still enough of a profit to finish paying Ellie's dad back and tuck a little away for later.

"Enough shop talk. How about another beer?" Kyle suggests.

"Sure thing." I glance around the restaurant area, which is starting to fill with bar patrons. I can't help but really appreciate this place. The architecture. The mixture of old and new. Wood and steel. Multiple levels, something for everyone. "I think I'll take my chances at the bar, place looks swamped," I comment, standing to go for the drinks.

"Some big performance tonight, I guess." Kyle shrugs.

Walking to the bar, I hold up my beer and two fingers, trying to get Chloe's attention. Jake finally let her get behind the bar. I laugh to myself at how overly eager she appears to be, but she seems to make all the regulars happy. It appears to be irritating the hell out of Jake.

The bar is standing room only now, completely packed. "Hey,

man!" I holler when I see Jake come around the corner. "Who's playing tonight?"

Jake turns to face me at the same time the crowd roars. He smiles but I can't hear what he's saying over the clapping and whistles. Then I hear the opening chords of a song begin to play, just a soft melody. But not just any song. I turn toward the stage and my eyes confirm what my heart already knows. It's the same one I heard in the park that day.

"It feels so good to be back at SPOTLIGHT!" Ellie croons into the mic. The crowd goes wild, my heart doing the same.

I can't believe it. She's back. Why wouldn't she tell me? If Kyle wouldn't have—

Kyle?

Shaking my head, not believing what I'm seeing, I turn to find my boss giving me a big thumbs up, wearing a cheesy-ass grin. Our table is now filled with his wife and the rest of the crew, people who are more than coworkers and friends, people who are like extended family. They pulled through for me when I needed them most.

Something jabs me in the ribs. "Damn!" I grab my side and look next to me. It's Rain.

"Surprise, lover boy." She wears a smile that honestly scares me a little.

"This was planned?" I ask, even though I already know the answer. She did this. She came back.

See you later.

Today is my later. Later is now.

"Well, duh!" Rain shouts over the crowd, which keeps getting louder the more Ellie talks about being back and missing home. "What are you waiting for?" she shouts after me. But I only hear one voice. *Hers.*

Get to her. *Now.*

Just knowing she is here I can't think straight. I push my way through the crowd; I can't get there fast enough. She is all I need.

It's her.

It's her.

It's her.

"And you know what I figured out while I was gone?" Ellie coos to the crowd, strumming her guitar as she catches me standing in the middle of the floor. Her breath hitches, her smile widens. "I can sing from anywhere in the world. I can write anywhere. Record almost anywhere. But there's only one place I'm inspired. Here. See there's this guy." She keeps strumming and every chord makes my heart beat louder. "He's not just any guy, he's *the* guy. I met him when I was performing, and he walked away." The crowd boos and I cringe, not sure where this is going. She smiles sweetly and continues, "Then I saw him again, right here in this very place. After falling in love, I was the one who walked away." The crowd gets quiet. "Not because I wanted to, but because he wanted me to. He was trying to be selfless and push me to follow my dreams, my heart. And I did." A lump forms in my throat.

"It led me back here. And this time, no one's walking away."

She may be talking to the crowd, but those words are for me. And I drink them in like a man dying of thirst as I inch my way closer, pulled by the sound of her voice saying words that mirror my feelings.

Ellie sets her guitar down and hops off the stage and just like some cheesy movie the crowd parts. I stand there mesmerized as she rushes into my arms. "I'm back!"

"About time." I begin to twirl her as the band starts to play.

"Wise men say, only fools rush in..."

I tense, but not because of the song.

"Lee, stay with me." Ellie reaches up for my face.

"Is that?" I can't believe what I'm hearing.

Ellie nods excitedly. "It's our moms."

Just six weeks ago, I would have been upset, scared, angry, hurt, but right now I can't help but feel happy. Everything happens for a reason and this girl, my girl, saved me from myself. Saved me from a world of regret and helped me to see forgiveness.

My mouth finds hers in a kiss that can only be described as coming home. Ignoring the catcalls, I grip her tighter, pulling her body against me. The house lights dim and everything else fades away as I hold her in my arms. My entire world.

My life.

"Welcome home baby," I murmur against her lips.

"It is, you know? My *home.*" Pressing my forehead against hers I look into her eyes. Eyes that are filling with tears. "You are my home, Presley Aaron Scott."

A blinding spotlight lands on us, and colors and smoke surround us on the dance floor.

"And you're mine, Ellie Hawthorne." I show her a promise of what's to come later with my lips.

I swear I hear Rain catcalling to get a room, which causes Ellie to giggle, the sound vibrating against my mouth. I lean back, so I can see my girl smile.

"You ready to go?" Ellie already has my hand in hers, pulling me along.

Yanking her back, I wrap my arms around her waist. "Did you just come from Nashville?"

"You know I did." Ellie is confused.

"I thought so." I wink. "Because you are the only ten-I-see."

Works every time.

The End

Acknowledgements

To all my readers - Forgiveness is a crazy thing. Sometimes we go our whole lives waiting for someone to ask for it. For the apology that never comes, but true forgiveness – comes from within. It doesn't have to be asked. An apology doesn't need to be said. We are in charge of when and if we decide to move on. So forgive yourself, forgive them, but most of all don't let the past control your *happiness*.

This book hit close to home with me. Even though I have never dealt with the same issues as Lee or Ellie, the meaning behind the story is still the same. Forgiveness. This book, did that for me. It made me see that it's my choice.

We choose to wake up happy, we choose who we are friends with, we choose what to eat each day. So why not choose to forgive?

I guess I have always known this. Hell, I'm sure I have given this advice a million times, but to actually practice what I preach? It's hard.

So, I did it. What I was dealing with? I forgave. I moved on and the peace I feel with it. It's good. I feel free.

So, thank you to these characters for changing my mind. This story – it was supposed to be sexy, flirty, fun and when I started to write – they put a stop to it. Lee and Ellie had something else in store for us. *For me.*

Thank you!

Cary xoxo

To my VIP Review Team – You guys rock! You have hand your hands in this book from the beginning. From naming the characters to spreading the word. Thank you for being on the team and for loving Lee and Ellie. xoxo #VIP #TeamWorkMakesTheDreamWork #IHeartYou

Brittany - What would I do without you? Thank you for being you! #BFF #TwinningIsWinning #CalmTheFuckDown

Stephanie – you whore! What can I say about you? You are the Timberlake to my Fallon. My Damon to my Kimmel. The end. #HippyShit #GirlsRule

Christy – (insert evil laugh here). #EnoughSaid #TalkSoup

Marla – thank you for being you! You worked around me when I changed it up so many times. This book has been crazy, but I promise you. It won't always be like that. xoxo #WinkWink

Let's not forget Spotify – Music is my life. Without it, I can't think. I can't write. I can't feel. My mood is my music or maybe music is my mood. Thank you Spotify! I will never leave you! You are my forever! #MusicIsLife

Last but not least... To my husband and kids – I love you guys so much. Thank you for your endless support. You picked up where I left off and brought me coffee, food and made sure I had time to focus on this story. I love you guys to the moon and back... I DID IT! Mommy's back!

About the Author

Cary Hart hails from the Midwest. A sassy, coffee drinking, sometimes sailor swearing, Spotify addict, lover of all things books!

When not pushing women down the stairs in the fictional world, Cary has her hands full. Soccer mom in all sense of the word to two wild and crazy, spoiled kiddos, and wife to the most supportive husband. In addition to writing full time, she enjoys binge watching Netflix, laying around in her hammock and baking up cookies for her family and friends.

Cary writes real, raw romance! In her stories the characters deal with life's everyday struggles and unwanted drama, they talk about the ugly and they become the broken. Everyone deserves a happy ending, but sometimes before you can appreciate the light, there has to be darkness.

Growing up, if someone would have told her she would become a writer, she wouldn't have believed them. It wasn't until she got her hands on her first romance novel, that the passion grew. Now she couldn't imagine her life any other way - she's living her dream.

To be the first to know of upcoming releases, please join:

Cary's Newsletter: **http://eepurl.com/cffmYX**

Or

Follow her on her website: **www.authorcaryhart.com**

Need to Find Cary? Send her an email:

caryhartbooks@gmail.com

Made in the USA
Lexington, KY
05 September 2018